THE "HAPPY" HUSTLER

Borgo Press Books by WILLIAM MALTESE:

Books for Other Presses:

THE "HAPPY" HUSTLER

by

WILLIAM MALTESE

THE BORGO PRESS

An Imprint of Wildside Press LLC

MMX

PART ONE

ME

PAUL...ET AL.

While, in retrospect, I can easily see that I was receiving money for sexual favors even during pre-pubescence, when I really didn't have a clue...and while I shall mention those incidents, herein, in passing, only since to leave them out would be to truncate my story of becoming, for the most part, a happy hustler...I have no intentions of going into the same explicit detail, in their regard, that I will do, in later chapters, when recounting my sexual encounters after I reached the age of consent. I have no desire to be accused of writing anything with even the slightest hint of seeming to pander to the prurient interests of pederasts.

So, just know that there was Donnie, the older boy, who lived next door, who enticed me with the offer of candy (yes, there is something behind that old ploy), to join him in the overly large doghouse (literally) usually occupied by his family's Great Dane, Pantegruel, when we weren't using it. While there was never any actual penile penetration, oral or anal, we did do a lot of petting and cuddling, Donnie physically spooning and stroking me from behind; which I've only now come to realize, has a sexual term that describes it—frottage—that always has me confusing it with *fromage*, French for cheese. By way of additional payment for my services, and silence, Donnie acted for years as my protector on the schoolyard.

There was Father Kinstock, the Catholic priest, who sucked my cock (which obliged him by going hard in his mouth but couldn't yet provide him even one drop of non-existent cream; he never seemed to mind), and who rewarded me with extra sacramental wine (Moganberry, I do believe).

There was the camp counselor, Jerry, who used to take me to bed (actually, "to cot") and caress me as if I were a cat he expected to purr (now, I suspect, he petted his big dick, as well), and who saw that I was never scheduled for any of the dirtier clean-up chores at Camp Winamacougaa.

There was the old pervert (at least he seemed old at the time), who tried to entice me into his car (I only started getting into cars later in life!), who ended up pulling out his dick and jacking it to messy conclusion while I watched through the open door of his auto that he kept slow-moving beside me. This particular instance wouldn't have fit within the parameters for retelling here, except that this guy did (as in apparent afterthought), punctuate his fast exit by tossing a twenty-dollar bill out the window which I retrieved and pocketed for a month's worth of ice cream.

There was good old Uncle Dack, on my mother's side, who took me into the shower with him at that SUV camping site, my parents and other members of our extended family having joined up for a weekend reunion, and spent a particularly long time soaping up my penis and his, afterwards providing me with a finger-to-his-lips *shhhhh, our secret,* and ten dollars in quarters for the park's arcade video games.

There was Coach Galen Jillins who masturbated while watching us young athletes in the Brankington Junior High School shower room. When I caught him, dick and cum in hand, no words were ever spoken about the incident, but I was suddenly relieved of all locker room duty for my next three years—at which time I graduated to high school.

Finally, there was Mr. Paul Fargunut, English teacher at Hellgintown High, who, upon my hearing rumors that he was gay, saw me go out of my way to charm him in order to raise my grade in his class from my deserved B to my undeserved A that I received at the "end of the day." All that was required was my allowing him a far less well-defined version of the frottage I'd perfected with Donnie, back in those Great Dane doghouse days. Mr. Fargunut merely liked, inadvertently, bumping up against me, during the course of the day, putting an occasional hand on my shoulder, and, once, brushing my tend-to-flop hair out of my eyes with his decidedly trembling hand.

None of the above left me either the least bit traumatized, or, years later, on the verge of (or actually into) a nervous breakdown. This doesn't mean that I'm demeaning any and all young men whose psyches have so obviously been fucked up by their having been fucked (around with) by older men at an early age. I'm merely saying that none of what happened to me, personally, ever seemed to leave me with anything other than an increased curiosity about my sexuality and about the sexuality of others; although, obviously it might have favorably skewered my way of thinking as regards just how sex can successfully be used as an item of barter.

In my rendition to follow, I'll mainly be dealing with young men, like myself, who I've met, and who seem to have coped far better with taking on hustling as a profession than have many of our peers. Once again, it's not that I don't think there aren't important stories to be told, and important lessons to be learned, from viewing, in an entirely negative light, many in our business; some male prostitutes not doing what they're doing because they want to but because they've been forced into it. It's just that there are two sides to every coin, and I choose, primarily, to deal, here, with the side of the hustling coin on which are found young men who have not only successfully evaded, for the most part, the horrible angst so often parse and parcel with our business, but who have actually thrived and succeeded, personally and financially, within it. There is already a plethora of books out there dealing with those countless poor souls who have become lost, wrecked and ruined, mentally and physically, from having offered up their cocks, mouths, and assholes for sale on the market place, without my adding this book to it.

THE TWO MR. WINS

Mr. Chad Win was another teacher of mine, this one of English Literature, at Hellgintown High. He was the first man I actively hustled after my balls officially dropped, my pubic hair sprouted, and I reached the age of consent that had me legally designated "a man."

I didn't start out to hustle Mr. Win. In fact, it would be wrong for anyone to assume that, at that stage of my life, I had already decided how thoroughly I would come to embrace the sex-for-hire life-style. I was actually still unsure of what I would do, career-wise, but tended toward marketing. Although I recognized, and it had been confirmed by certain of my teachers, as well, that I had a definite talent for writing, I never contemplated writing novels, or short stories, for a living. A Hemingway or Steinbeck wasn't who I thought I was, or who I ever aspired to be. While writing a book wasn't out of the question, one day, I figured it might be done, if ever, as a hobby, while I focused mainly on writing jingles, or tag lines, for products and merchandise, as an employee of some big-city advertising agency.

While I knew I wanted to go to college, and I knew my parents wanted me to go…and while I had always worked diligently to make my grades good enough for it to happen—whether by actually studying, or by letting Mr. Fargunut do a bit of brushing up against me in his classroom ...the specifics of where and when were still pretty much up in the air. Loans, scholarships, even summer jobs, still had to be looked into, with decisions to be made as to whether I would go immediately to a community college, or take off a year to get the tuition necessary for a larger, more prestigious university. On no account did I see Mr. Win, because of his connections, about which I didn't have a clue—even more so, because of the connections of his father, about which I had even less of a clue—being instrumental in pulling all of the strings necessary to make my wildest dreams of a higher education come true.

All I really wanted from Mr. Win was to see his dick, because I'd heard it was such a really big one; and, I wanted to see if it was true that his cock was so big that he could actually suck it, himself, merely by bending from his waist, whether sitting or standing, opening his mouth wide, and swallowing the monster all of the way down to its thick roots. As usual, then as now, the idea of "having sex" wasn't anything I genuinely felt a desperate need to have happen. If it did happen, though, in the case of Mr. Win, in the course of my getting to see his big dick, and whether or not he could eat it, I had no qualms about sex happening. By, then, I'd had more than one cock fucked up my ass, and I'd sucked on more than one dick. Besides which, Mr. Win wasn't, then, or now, hard to look at. He has brown hair, brown eyes, square jaw, athletic body, and looked, in those days, Ivy-League even when wasn't wearing his *Harvard Yard* sweat shirt.

All of my friends, gay and straight, had heard the rumor about his exceptional sexual endowment, but no one I knew had ever actually seen it. It was always someone who knew someone who knew someone-who-had-choked-on-it.

My quest, then, was either to prove the rumor true, or, once and for all, to prove the rumor untrue. The problem, of course, was that Mr. Win seemed to make it a point never to screw around with any of his students, even when, and if, one or more of them, even if above the age of consent, approached him and blatantly made it obvious to him that their bodies were sexually available to him for his taking.

I discarded the obviousness of running into him in the *BelleBoy* unisex bar, where we all knew he hung out after school and on most weekends, and went in search of him in other places, not gay- or school-related, where I might find him on his off hours.

I started bumping into him (once, quite literally) during the intermissions of the symphony, opera, and local civic theater. Surprisingly, what resulted was a bona-fide friendship from assumed mutual interests that had nothing whatsoever to do with sex, except that it had been initiated by my desire to see what Mr. Win had in his pants and whether or not he could eat it.

I met his mother and his father who were even more involved in the cultural scene than he was. Suddenly, I was invited to gallery openings, or after-performance fetes that someone or other was throwing for the cast of some opera or play in local production.

All of which led not to sex with Mr. Win, but to the eventual decision by him and his father, the elder Mr. Win, to pull the strings necessary to get me into their alma mater—as well as provide the scholarship—actually, two—that would take care of all my tuition and book fees.

To this day, I've never seen either of the Mr. Wins completely naked, with no idea as to whether or not the younger's dick is the monster that so many people still believe that it is. Certainly, I have no clue whether the younger's self-fellatio skills are what they're supposed to be. My only sex with him has proved, over the years, to be merely in my fantasies. Fantasies, as I've discovered are, pretty much, always preferable to the real thing, anyway.

I used to come home from the symphony, or some play, and head to my room, strip down on my bed, and imagine that Mr. Win (always the younger) had returned with me (or, that we'd gone to his place).

"I've been waiting a long time to take a look at that supposedly big dick of yours," I'd always say. "What say you give me a peek, here and now?"

At which point, he'd stand up, unzip (or unbutton) the crotch of whatever pants he was wearing at the time, send his right hand into the breach, as well as through the front opening of any underwear he had on—usually by some major designer, like Draqual—and proceed to reel out his truly magnificent and gargantuan phallic monster. As big as I always imagined it, I suspect that, if it had really been that large, it would have readily provided more evidence, beneath his trousers, than it ever did. Actually, while I looked often enough, in my attempt to discover evidence of his penis, its shape, and its size, beyond the concealing material of his usually (purposely?) baggy pants, there was only one time when I actually thought I succeeded…only to decide, quickly, that there was no way anyone, even Mr. Win, could really sport a cock that humungous.

Anyway, his cock out, in my fantasies, the next bit of natural progression, was my asking, "Is it true you can really suck it?"

By which time, I'd have my cock in my hand, a tad embarrassed by even its usually impressive size so dwarfed by Mr. Win's massive erection, and I'd be beating away on my dick, like crazy.

"Want me to give eating my dick a try, just for your look-see?" Mr. Win would ask.

"Yes, please, and thank-you," I'd reply, not waiting for him to start before my fist was pounding all the faster, up and over, up and down, the shaft of my stiff dick.

He'd play his prick to a harder state which, unbelievably, always made it even bigger.

"Good, God, Mr. Win!" I'd exclaim. "You must have to go to the elephant barn of the zoo to find an asshole big enough to take that on."

"Oh, it'll fit up your asshole just as nicely as it does up any elephant," he'd say. "Should we give it a try, as soon as I take a few minutes, here, to lube it up with some juicy spit of my own making?"

"Yes, Jesus, yes." My ass would bounce on the bed, by then, so fucking fast that I'd always think my parents would soon shout up the stairs to find out what in the hell all of the mattress springs' squeaking was all about..

Then, Mr. Win would do it: suck his dick, easy as you—he—pleased. Just bend over, hold his hard dick in position with both of his hands, open his mouth wide, and spike his head, via his mouth and into his throat, with that monster dick of his. Not even a pause in his long lip-lock slide from his fist-size cock corona to his thick cock roots. His chin pressed tightly into his lower hairy belly, his nose socked tightly in against his hairy balls.

I'd bust a nut and send my cum flying, sometimes blasting my body all of the way to my face where a lick of my tongue could, would, and did, capture samples of it.

THEO AND TOM

My first year in college, I roomed in a dorm with Theo Maze whose parents, coincidentally enough, had a Kansas farm that grew maize.

By my second year in college, the two Mr. Wins, having determined that I was apparently suited to university life, and that I was, indeed, prepared to hang in there for the long haul, decided that fraternity life was of vital networking opportunity for any young man, including me, and made it happen. My leaving Theo wasn't any big deal, because he'd become genuinely withdrawn and downright secretive during the school year I knew him.

After first meeting, I became a tad confused. Theo obviously entered university at one helluva better financial advantage than I did, or so it seemed at first glance; even he admitted, early on, that the family farm was a money-maker, his old man raking in the profits, hands over fists, from the corn crop. That said, I always seemed to have more spending money than he did, finally eliciting his confession that his old man, rolling in money, or not, was a tight wad, in the extreme, as well as a control freak, who, assuming Theo would one day take over the family business (which Theo wasn't all that keen to do), saw putting his son through college, especially such an expensive one, as an extravagance and waste of both time, money, and effort.

For the first six months I knew Theo, he was frequently borrowing money from me. Then, he began disappearing each and every weekend, returning with enough cash not only to pay me back what he owed me, but to begin some serious partying on his own. He said he'd lucked out with a part-time job in the nearby major city, but he remained vague as to what kind of job, and with whom. In fact, he remained so evasive that my natural curiosity got the better of me, and, one weekend, I actually followed him from university into the city.

Feeling very much like Sherlock Holmes and silly as a result, I watched him park his car on a night-time downtown street and walk several blocks to take up a rather provocative pose (sole of his left foot back against a building's dirty brick wall, his hips thrust forward). Even as I watched, he grabbed a handful of the t-shirt he was wearing, gave a forceful tug, and ripped it so that it did very little, any longer, by way of covering his admittedly very impressive chest.

Ten minutes later, a car stopped. Theo walked over to it, leaned into its open window on the driver's side, had a bit of a chat with the driver, and a quick walk-around around to climb on in.

I assumed he'd pre-planned the meeting, and I was suddenly at a loss. If my first inclination was to keep on following, and see what they were up to, my car was parked near Theo's, a few blocks back, and definitely wasn't convenient for any successful continuance of my tail. So, I just stood there, temporarily uncertain as to just what in the hell I should do next, when a car pulled up and stopped at the curb less than five feet from me.

I thought I'd been caught, by Theo, or by his friend, in the act of spying, they having circled the block to confront me. I was still trying to figure out how I was going to explain my being where I was when the car window slid down, and I didn't see hide or hair of Theo anywhere inside.

Nor did I recognize the driver. He was a well-put-together business-type who looked as if he might have come straight from the office. He had short-cut graying-brown hair. His eyes were dark, their exact color not readily discernable in the dim lighting. He was clean-shaven, with a nicely squared jaw line and a slight cleft dead-center his chin. He wore his suit very well; it was obviously expensive.

"How's it going?" he asked, as if he knew me from somewhere; although, I would have remembered him, I'm sure.

"Going fine, thanks," I said. "You?"

"Always delighted to see new talent," he said.

Talent? Did he expect me to sing and dance?

"You *are* new, right?" he carried on.

"Right."

"Looking for a little action?"

"Maybe." Suddenly, remembering that long-ago guy who offered me candy, I had a sudden epiphany as to how Theo might be making extra money on the side. Curious as to whether or not I had it figured right, I said, "How about you?"

"How about you suck my cock," he came right out and said. "Then, we won't have to worry about me wearing a rubber, will we?"

I'd heard that AIDS wasn't likely to be passed on during a blowjob, but was I really convinced of that?

"I don't know," I said. "You can't be too careful, these days."

"Tell you what," he said. "You face-ride my cock, bareback, and I'll pay you…." He quoted a price that had me thinking that Theo wouldn't have to suck too many dicks, bareback, to tell his father to fuck off.

"Okay," I said. I was a bit more daring-do, then, than I'd been when candy-man asked me into his car, all those years before, and I'd refused him. I'd had a few martial arts classes, since then, and given a few blowjobs, and I felt pretty confident I could handle myself with Mr. Businessman, and his cock, even if either tried anything funny.

I admit to being turned on by the idea of providing sex for money. While this wasn't the first time in my life I'd hustled for recompense, as previously mentioned, it was the first time I'd come into it really knowing for sure that I would be providing hard-core sex for cold cash.

"You have a room?" I asked. "It's either that, or we drive back to my dorm at the university." Something told me that Theo, as usual, would be sucking and fucking that night, and the next, before he did his regular early-morning Monday show-up, shower, and groggy-headed mosey off to classes. "It'll take us a little time to get there."

"Ah, a fresh schoolboy!" he said and sounded as if that pleased him. "Out for a little spending money, are you?"

"Out for a *lot* of spending money," I said; in for a penny, in for a pound; in for a cent, in for a dollar.

"Come on around and get in, then," he said. "We don't need a room. I know a place where we can park, and you can do me right here in the car."

As soon as I was seated beside him, he handed me my money, up front, which any experienced hustler, I've since learned, would have demanded happen. Luckily, Tom (that's his name) wasn't new to buying prime beef off the town's meat rack, and he knew the rules of the game far better than I did.

I was enveloped within the sensuous smell of leather. I thought it was the plush car upholstery that seemed specifically to mold my back and backside, like one of those form-fitting chairs in sci-fi films. As it turned out, though, it was mainly Tom's cologne. As I was soon to discover, too, even his big cock smelled erotically of it.

I was to get my first look at this first cock I'd ever been paid to suck after we pulled up and stopped in a very dark alleyway, between two deserted warehouses, in the industrial part of the city. The outside scenario was perfect for one of those horror flicks, zombies on the loose; inside the car, though, it was cozy and smelling mighty fine.

Tom unfastened the crotch of his trousers and made his first valiant attempt to get his cock into view; its stiffness prevented it from immediately making its appearance through the inadequate breach of material its owner had provided for it.

"This may take a minute," he said. "Please bear with me. Sometimes, when I luck out with a very exceptionally handsome young man, like you, my cock reacts by getting so damned stiff that it needs a bit of additional coaxing to come out and play."

While he unfastened his belt, and undid the top button of his trousers' waistband, allowing the flaps of his pants crotch to fillet and give me my first real look at his pretty-perfect dick, thrust as it already was through the front opening of his impeccably white boxer undershorts, I wondered if Theo had ever had to wait those extra seconds before he'd deep-dived Tom's big dick. (I found out later that the two never had managed to hook up).

I was anxious to get at his steely erection, not so much because I had this undeniable need to feel and taste it shoved deeply into my face, but because I wondered just how well my sucking on it was going to stack up against all of the really professional cock-sucking mouths there before mine.

"You have a preference as to how you'd like this to go down?" I asked. I'd already learned, quite aside from hustling, that if you have a way you like to get sucked or fucked, or be sucked or fucked, you save you and your partner, and/or partners, a helluva lot of needless experimentation, time, and bother, by merely spelling it out from the get-go. "You want me concentrating on that bulbous cock head, or do you prefer some hearty deep-throat from the outset?"

I swear to God, his cock commenced three quick jerks, and its eye literally squirted pre-cum that, up until then, I'd only seen emerge a cock, including my own, as ooze.

"I do like a pro who knows his business," Tom said. "So, why don't you just munch on my cock head for awhile, and do some deep-sixing of the whole thing when I give you the go-ahead?"

So, my left hand took hold of his stiff shaft, and my right hand did some palming of his more-than-a-handful nuts. My mouth opened wide over the cap of his erection, and my lips slid down and over his cock head to an immediate lock just beneath his cock's coronal flare. My head tilted slightly to the left, in order to provide his cock's g-spot (where belly met crown), with more substantial contact with the inside of my cheek.

I sucked, chewed, and heartily gobbled the top of his boner, pleased as all hell when he started making little mewls, grunts, and groans, which told me that, whatever I was doing, I was doing it right. Whenever I heard him express an exceptionally loud voicing of his appreciation, I made sure soon to repeat whatever it was that had caused his response in the first place.

Frankly, I was surprised by just how fast my sucking off just the tip of his thick dick got him so really turned on. I'd later be amused, no end, to learn that it had happened because he had genuinely thought he finally had a head swinging on his dick that had somehow been specifically trained by a bona-fide professional to do what it was doing.

"Goddamn, kid, take it all!" he bellowed and put both of his hands to my head and gave the forceful push that slid my face all of the way from his sucked cock head to the base of his dick. Good thing I'd dealt with anxious guys before, or I would have choked for sure. As it was, he got what he wanted without me even providing the slightest gag reflex. What I did provide was some automatic swallows that fluttered my throat tightly against the total length of his dick and did some serious and sensuous massaging.

"Jesus, fuck!" he said and surprised the holy hell out of me by shooting his hot cummy load, right then and there. As I sucked all of it away, I thought that was the shortest time I'd ever had to work for a substantial paycheck. Once again, I was computing just how many cocks that Theo (or I?) could take on, during any one weekend. Hell, Theo would soon be financially independent of his old man and from the far-more-work-required-than-this corn crop back home.

While neither Tom nor I ever started out that evening ever expecting it to extend beyond that initial blowjob, it ended up lasting all of the way up to and through most of my senior year, ceasing only, in the middle of my last semester, when Tom was transferred, by his company, to its Dubai office. We remain friends to this day, and, whenever we find ourselves close by, we invariably end up renewing old times by my going down on his perfect dick, and by him paying me for his pleasure in my doing so.

GARY

I didn't capitalize upon my initial success, as an assumed pro cocksucker of Tom's cock, by taking up permanent weekend residence on that city's meat rack. Having found what it was all about, I had no real desire to pursue its possibilities, let alone hamper Theo's style by frequently showing up there; my curiosity, as regards how it might be to get into a car, eat cock, and get paid for it, had been satisfied. While, as a mere student, I wasn't exactly rolling in cash, I'd never really been hurting from lack of it, what with all of my university expenses pretty much paid, and my parents regularly sending me an allowance. I had even less of a cash-flow problem after taking on Tom and his dick as paying regulars; even with Tom, though, I quickly came to think it really too inconvenient for me to continue making trips into the city, once a week; it was Tom's idea that he start checking in weekly at one of the hotels adjacent to the university that usually are booked by family members stopping by to say hello to their student off-springs.

When Tom suggested that I expand my clientele by even one, I, at first, actually said, "Thanks but no thanks!" Not exactly with a genius IQ, I did know I was managing just fine with all of my classes, but that didn't mean that I could coast through any of them; they required a good deal of study. No way did I have any intentions of disappointing my parents, the two Mr. Wins, even me, by flunking out of school, especially just because I'd been offered another cock to suck and the additional cold cash that would come with sucking it. I still saw my career as in advertising/marketing, not in peddling various parts of my anatomy for the sexual amusement of others. While I had done the mental computations that figured out the money that could possibly be made by someone (Theo? me?), genuinely motivated to eat three or four dicks a night, even fuck an asshole or two, and/or assume the position to take it up the ass once, or twice, or thrice, during the course of any one evening, I never really seriously looked upon any of that as having actual profession potential, any more than I actually believed it was any real intention, in the long run, of Theo to earn his living from any other means than selling the corn his family had been selling for generations on end.

"All work and no play...," Tom said, by way of additional persuasion for me to take on Gary who Tom had told of my "incredible expertise." Gary was anxious to try it out, and pay for the trying.

Maybe I would have been sooner to agree if I ever genuinely looked upon sex as "play." While it could be fun, always to a certain degree, and while there was always enjoyment to be had in every orgasm and, even, in seeing if I could provide someone else with a never-to-be-forgotten orgasm, it was usually just more effort than it was worth. Most of the time, I even ate Tom's cock not so much because I enjoyed it but because I enjoyed Tom. He turned out to be clever, erudite, and amusing. There is nothing I find sexier, in a man or in a woman, than his or her ability to make me laugh.

That I finally agreed to give Gary a go—one time only, or so I thought at the time—was because Tom ended up, next time, asking me to fuck his friend after Tom had provided me not only with a very enjoyable dinner but with several good laughs. Both of which put me in a vulnerably good mood; content, too, in knowing I'd just that afternoon aced a very crucial biology lab test.

"Gary will crack you up, I promise," Tom said. "Just wait and see. And if his time with you sees him ready to finalize the contract his company presently has pending with mine, then, there may even be a little extra cash in it for you."

"Please tell me you're not really counting upon pimping my fucking skills to persuade Gary into coming through for you on some kind of genuine business deal," I complained. Tom continued to believe I was a pro at hustling, no matter what I said, or what I did, that directly contradicted his false assumption. If Gary came into this expecting me to put out like the pro Tom promised, and I merely came across the schoolboy I was, eminent disaster might loom on the horizon.

"Don't worry," Tom assured. "Just follow along with Gary, no matter how bizarre, and you'll be just fine."

"Bizarre?" That was the first time he'd inserted "bizarre" into our conversation. "How bizarre?"

"Fun-bizarre," he managed finally. I promise that he will not be asking you to tie him to the bed, while you're wearing Gucci riding boots, and wielding a whip to turn his ass all bloody and make him mutter the 'stop' word. Although if you think you might like to give that a try, I do know someone I think would...."

He stopped talking when I waved off even the idea of whatever B&D he was suggesting. Obviously, he continued to labor under the misconception that I knew far more, and had done far more, than I really knew, had ever done, or—at that time in my life—figured I'd ever know, or ever do.

"I would really prefer that you be more specific, as regards to what I should expect from Gary."

He told me.

I told him that I thought not.

He told me about Gary, and "another hustler" and a party. He had me laughing until I cried.

This, in turn, had me waiting in the hotel room, on the university outskirts, on the night Gary came knocking.

He arrived with two large plastic bags, one of which he handed over to me as soon as he was sure he had the right room and the right young man.

"Bathroom through there," I pointed him and his bag in the right direction.

I dumped the contents of my assigned bag out on the bed. I still couldn't believe I was about to do what I was about to do; except, I was undeniably attracted to the novelty of it.

Gary rapped on the inside of the bathroom door and asked if I was ready.

"Give me another minute or so, buddy," I requested. A zipper had stuck, and I was in the process of trying to coax it open. It was so crucially placed that having it stay stuck would have been a major complication.

Finally, I achieved success, and I carefully tested to make sure the fix wasn't just temporary.

"Ready?" Gary asked again; I tried to determine if he sounded anxious or merely muffled.

"Ready." I said. At least, I was as ready as I figured I'd ever be.

The bathroom door handle dipped, and the door came open; Gary stepped into the bedroom.

Not that I would have ever recognized the huge fuzzy bunny rabbit as the man who had arrived and carried his bag into the bathroom.

I almost laughed aloud. The two of us—Peter Cotton Tail, and the Easter Bunny?—looked downright ridiculous; except, Tom had made me promise not to laugh. "Furries take themselves and what they do very seriously," he'd said and had started laughing; I had joined in; neither of us stopped until our sides ached.

At least, I didn't have to say anything; Gary wouldn't hear the quiver in my almost-laugh-aloud voice. In that, rabbits didn't talk, did they? Rabbits were only known for about five things: delivering candy eggs, twitching their noses, eating an occasional carrot or two, saying, "What's up, Doc?", and shitting little pellets of poo.

I came at him, hard and fast. Forgetting that my costume extended outward from my body, I hit him before I knew it, and I did so decidedly harder than I intended. We were both embedded within so much padding that we were like two Japanese sumo wrestlers colliding in the ring. The stomach of my costume concaved; so did his; both rebounded in a way that sent us in opposite directions, like two identical magnetic poles lined up on each other in a science lab.

I tried to get back at him, but I couldn't see a fucking thing! Not only was my rabbit's head too big, its eye holes continually tilting to provide me no view but the inside of the head, but, whenever I was able to see through the holes, then one or both ears, each with its own peculiar wrong-way flop, drooped to impede my vision.

What's more, I kept tripping over my feet. It was as if I was wearing those humungous feet worn by clowns, or—tah-dah!—big, floppy, bunny slippers.

Literally, I was banging off the walls, grabbing for support that, nine times out of ten, wasn't there.

I began sweating like the proverbial stuck pig; although, someone once told me that real pigs, stuck or otherwise, don't sweat. I had perspiration drooling into my eyes; I couldn't see even at those rare moments when my eyeholes were properly aligned and my fake ears were out of the way. Rivers of sticky wet ran my neck, down the center of my chest, onto the floodplain of my belly. It cascaded within the crack of my ass.

God only knows how I finally caught Bunny Gary in that mad chase around that hotel room. Surely, he must have gone specifically out of his way to be found, or it would never have happened. Surely, what I was supposed to do would never have gotten done, if I'd been left to get it done on my own. I would have been the only rabbit in hutch history unable to rabbit-fuck because I was stumbling around without a clue as to how to make it happen.

Gary's ass suddenly butted up against my lap and almost toppled me over backwards. Certainly, it disoriented me enough so that I had to think really hard about what had happened, what was happening, and even what would happen. Then, I genuinely panicked when I thought the zipper at the crotch of my bunny suit was stuck shut, for not the first time.

My loud gasp resulted from a combination of the claustrophobia I felt, all hemmed in, on all sides, by what I suspect, now, was real rabbit fur; by success in getting the zipped zipper unzipped; and, by shock at just how cool the air of the room felt as it rushed into the breach of my crotch-opened costume to meet up with all the sweat that veneered every damned inch of the naked me inside that costume.

God knows how my cock managed to get outside my costume and inside Gary's ass; suddenly, it just was. I was hunched over Gary; I was holding to his bunny midsection with my front bunny legs; my bunny head was laid upon his bunny back; and, I was rabbit-fucking his rabbit butt with my rabbit cock, like all holy hell.

I'm sure it's one of those things people always say they have to see to believe. That's not true, though, because, through whatever miraculous conjuration of the Zodiac that allowed my eyeholes properly to align, simultaneous to my ears properly flopping in the right directions, and my sweat stopping, for one quick second, its blinding of eyes, I actually did catch a glimpse of the two of us—Bunny Gary, Bunny Me—as reflected back to me from the large hotel mirror that hung one wall. The vision was so unbelievably unreal and bizarre-funny that I couldn't stop my bubbling inclination to burst into loud and raucous laughter. The harder I tried to suppress the inclination to laugh out loud, the more the urge became dominant.

My orgasm, which occurred during my hysteria, was cataclysmic and rocked my poor bunny body to the core of my poor bunny being.

All the while I fed my bullets of bunny cum deep up Gary's bunny butt, I couldn't stop humping. My hips kept on automatic pilot...pumping, pumping, and pumping some more.

Both Gary and I made noisy and guttural grunting sounds that would have been completely unfamiliar to anyone in a truly bunny world, but which any pig would have recognized right away.

JAY

"Do this one as a favor to you," Tom said.

"You do remember that I'm really just a schoolboy, don't you?" I said. "What with you, and an occasional session of dress-up with Gary, and with all of my studies and school activities, I'm just really not sure I can really squeeze—Jay, is it?—into my schedule."

"Actually, it'll be your stiff boner trying to squeeze into Jay's tight asshole," Tom reminded, "while you read him a verse or two of Edgar Allen Poe poetry from a book opened across his bare back."

I shake my head at the strange things people do in the bedroom.

"I'm just trying my best to budget what little time I seem to have available for everything I have to do, these days," I waffled, "and still get a degree."

"Well, I'll be out of town this next weekend, on business, which should at least provide a solution, time-wise, for clearing a space in your schedule for Jay, just this one time, maybe, yes?"

"And I should make the effort, instead of studying, just why?"

"He's a literary agent. You did say you were a writer, writing a book, didn't you?"

"I said I was a university student, trying his best to pass his classes, planning to go into marketing/advertising, and one day, maybe, writing a book as a kind of something done on the side."

"Did you, or did you not tell me, you are writing a book even now?"

"It's merely a relaxing pastime to which I've not found much time to add anything, lately."

"Poor, baby!" he sounded less than sympathetic.

"I can't imagine the guy even considering taking on someone who doesn't have more of a track record than I do," I said.

"Don't try modesty with me. I've vouched for your wizardry in bed."

"I was referring to his taking me on as in a literary capacity," I explained what didn't really need explaining, "not to his taking me and my cock on for a butt-fuck."

"Jay handles a lot of authors who write hot stuff. Remember that best-seller, last year, *The Emperor Ming's Courtesan*? The author is one of his. I'll bet you could out-write that book's sex scenes in a heartbeat."

"My book-in-progress is about the Apocalypse, not about screwing."

"You know the old adage about never knowing if your ship is going to come in unless you first set it to sail?"

"I do now."

"Think about it. Opportunity is knocking; just asking you to do a bit of 'knocking' in return. You have someone, here, who is genuinely interested, granted not initially so much in your writing skills, which I suspect are as stupendous as your sexual skills, but who's certainly someone for you to know in the future, should you ever decide to take your writing beyond its hobby stage."

I gave fucking, or not fucking, Jay some more thought. In the end, I said, yes…likely, I thought, it would be just that once…no guarantees for repeats, even if Jay was bowled over by my fucking and recitation skills, which, still considering myself a rank amateur in the field of sexuality, I very much doubted would really be the case, no matter how enthusiastic Tom and Gary were about my performances in the bedroom.

Once again, it wasn't the sex, or the money for sex, that won me over, as much as it was my curiosity as to how two people actually managed the logistics of the sex Jay required: someone (me?) fucking him and reading Edgar Allen Poe poetry at one and the same time. Actually, as soon as I got back to the dorm, Theo off as usual, getting fucked or sucked, or fucking and sucking, I did a bit of experimenting by way of reading while I jacked off. Since I didn't have any Poe handy, I made due with my Business Law text. Actually, I was quite pleased by how, just by concentrating, I could pretty much keep my enunciation fairly clear and concise up to and including while my cum was filling my hand. Of course, I'd have to find out, somehow, if it was really the precise oratory Jay was interested in hearing, or a more garbled rendition supposedly distorted by all the pleasure I was being provided by Jay's tightly gripping asshole.

By way of additional preparation, I checked a volume of Poe's poetry out of the university library, providing myself with a backup volume, just in case Jay didn't bring a book of his own.

Of course, he had been doing what he was doing long enough to know he'd better bring along his own copy of any poetry he wanted read, or risk finding himself with a hot and eager fucker but with none of Jay's favorite poetry for that hot and eager fucker to read.

Was I a hot and eager fucker when I showed up at Jay's hotel door, and he let me in? Answer: I was more eager than I was hot. Again, I was more interested in how this all might work, if it worked out at all. Certainly, though, I was hot enough so that I arrived if not with my boner in hand, then, at least with it in my pants; although, to be quite frank, I could, then, and can, now, pretty much summon a stiffy, on command, no matter what the circumstances.

Jay isn't the most appetizing man I've ever fucked. His black hair seems too "puffy" and too tightly curled. His head seems too big. His eyebrows seem too thick. His nose seems too big. His lips seem too thick. His torso and arms seems too long; his legs seem too bowed and too short. His feet seem too big. Chimpanzee-like comes most immediately to mind, especially with the tufts of course black hair protruding through the space provided at his neck by his open shirt collar (he has hair all over his chest, belly, chest, legs, crotch, and ass; his back surprisingly clean of it—maybe because so many books, riding there, have worn it away?). His expensive suit (I could tell by its label) was ill-fitting.

Nor was I sure that he was all that impressed by me, since he stepped into the room, his volume of Poe clamped to his chest as if I might steal it, and immediately sat down in a chair, motioned me into the chair across from him, and, instead of stripping down for sex, assumed the role of literary agent interviewing a potential client.

"Tom tells me you're writing a book."

I was embarrassed as all hell that he had arrived, somehow having actually taken Tom's comments on my literary aspirations as valid.

"Isn't everyone?" I asked, trying to make light of it.

"No," he said, surprisingly serious, or at least coming across that way. "Everyone is merely *thinking* he or she can write a book. Not many really do it. Not many who do do it do it well. Tom is genuinely impressed by what he's read of yours."

Except, Tom hadn't read anything I'd written.

"Tom is possibly a tad biased," I suggested.

"Maybe so," he conceded; I was genuinely impressed that he wasn't quick to discard that possibility. "Then, again, you certainly come highly recommended as an authority on the subject matter."

I was confused. "On the Apocalypse?"

"I'm sorry?" He was obviously as confused as I was.

"That's what my book is about."

His face screwed up, making him all the more unattractive. "I was told it was of a highly sexual nature."

I could have jumped in with the old bit about it being unwise to assume anything, in that it made an "ass" out of "u" and "me", but I didn't. The poor guy had every reason to be perplexed.

"I've merely been thinking of writing something of a highly sexual nature," I attempted to cover my ass and

Tom's—before covering Jay's ass with my cock and cupping lap, if he ever began showing any real interest in having that happen.

"Ahhhh," he said, evidently pleased that I'd made sense of what had been on the verge of a total misunderstanding. "Something on college-campus promiscuity among homosexual male students would be of particular interest. Say, 20,000 words? If, that is, you can manage them within the next couple of months. There's an anthology in the works, by a publisher with which I've always had a close working relationship, and, while I can't guarantee your work placement in it, I'd certainly be willing to take a look at whatever you can give me that might fit that particular niche."

"Speaking of niches to be filled?" I parried. It would only be later that I decided to set that particular literary ship to sail, surprised as all hell when it actually came in as one of the detours that would keep me forever from any 9 to 5 job in any advertising agency. In the meantime… "Have you chosen the particular Poe piece you want me to read?"

He placed the book in his lap, opened it. He removed his business card—x-marks-the-spot—and handed it to me. "Do keep that," he said.

I put his card in my pocket and reached for the book he extended in its wake.

"Ah, *The Raven*," I said, "one of my favorites." Nor was I lying. While I've never really been a particular fan of poetry, especially the kind that doesn't rhyme (prose?), Poe's efforts, from my earliest acquaintance with them, are pretty much the most enjoyable I've found. "Before we begin, though…."

I stood, placed the opened book on the nearby tabletop and began to undress.

"Yes, of course," he agreed and stood, seeming far more nervous than I would have expected from someone who had been through this far more times than I had.

His unbuttoned shirt revealed more of the thick matting of hair that covers his pasty-pudding chest and love-handle tummy. By comparison, my chest is hairless, and, if not thickly muscled, then, enough so that Tom often flatters me by saying I could have modeled for Praxiteles and seen that sculptor well-pleased.

"I do think it imperative, Jay, that I ask, before we get started, whether or not your intention is to have me provide you with a clearly articulated rendering of Poe's work, or with guttural accompaniment, as our session progresses towards its conclusion."

He stopped unbuckling his pants and looked genuinely surprised. This, in turn, had me surprised, in that I couldn't believe I was the first person who had ever asked him that question; although it turned out, that was exactly the case.

"Tom did say you were a professional," he said finally, "and how extremely professional of you to ask. The truth is, though, that I'm not sure I really have an answer for you, or have really given it much thought; probably because I'm not really sure, even with the help of my psychiatrist, just why I've found my way to this specific sexual proclivity. Clarity in the readers' readings really hasn't seemed to matter, in the past, possibly because I know most of Poe's work by heart. That said, clarity, especially toward the end, is so seldom managed, I'd certainly be interested in hearing if you can make that happen or, at least, come close."

"No guarantees," I said, although practice had assured me that, at least with my cock in my hand, I could pretty much keep each word of a poem recognizable, in a pinch; cock fucking his hairy ass might be something else again, "but since you hopefully won't be too disappointed if I fail, I'll give it the old college try."

I smiled at my little pun, regarding "college", considering who I was, and where we were. He obliged by smiling back and seeming far more at ease than he'd been on his arrival.

"And, do you want this to be on the floor, or on the bed?" I was hoping for the former, if just because of the more difficult logistics involved in keeping a book in place while fucking on flexible bedsprings, not even adding into that equation how impending orgasms have a tendency to put those participating into all sorts of gyrations, swings, and sways."

"Dog-style on the floor has always seemed best," he gave me the answer for which I'd hoped. So far, so good!

When we were both stripped naked, Jay got down on his hands and knees and presented his hairless back for placement, on, of the Poe volume, and his hairy ass for placement, in, of my stiff dick. I obliged him with the former, opened; front, spine, and back down and balanced, while I knelt down behind him, my left hand steadying the book, my right hand fisting my dick.

Once I kneeled into position, my left hand kept on the book, and my right hand eased my cock head into Jay's ass crack at the base of his spine. After which, I performed a series of back-and-forth hip movements that initially only blunted my cock against the run of his anal valley, until finally....

"Ohhhhh," he moaned lowly; I knew, from that, as well as from the suddenly pliant qualities of the spot against which my cock was pressed, that I was finally successfully aligned for pushing my meat into and up Jay's asshole.

"Once upon a midnight dreary," I recited, putting more pressure behind another of my forward hip movements to concave his anal pucker and, then..."while I pondered weak and weary"...slowly, but surely, to roll open his sphincter, like a camera lens, to let my cock slide inside... "over many quaint and curious volumes of forgotten lore ..." and to have our fuck and poetry reading officially begun.

As I continued reading, while simultaneously pushing my cock into place, I was surprised by how quickly I coordinated both. Since I didn't really find Jay's asshole, then and there, any more pleasurable than my hand had been, during practice sessions, it was merely a case of making sure that the book didn't slip and slide, or that I suddenly lost my place in reading the poem. The former was easily achieved in my early discovery that I could hook the outside edges of the book with the tips of my thumbs, my hands anchored to the convenient extra belly flesh of his love handles, and keep the volume pretty much in place, even though, even without doing that, his back seemed more than adequately wide by way of providing enough reading-stand accommodation.

Once my cock was slowly slid in all of the way, I slowly pulled it out to its head, while doing my best in my ongoing pronouncements of Poe's famous poem. When the head of my dick was the only part of my erection once again wrapped by the moue of his tight anal opening, it was merely a case of my sticking my just exited cock right back in, and, then, slowly, repeating it all, over again.

"And the silken sad uncertain rustling of each purple curtain...thrilled me—filled me with fantastic terrors, never felt before; So that now, to still the beating of my heart, I stood repeating: 'Tis some visitor entreating entrance at my chamber door...."

Definitely, I had the knack for doing what I was doing, without fumbling a word, and without missing a fuck-beat.

All along, Jay provided sound-effects. They began as little breathless sighs, became low grunts and growls, and, eventually, morphed into soft verbal accompaniment with the very same words of the poem I was speaking to him at the time. As the fuck and the reading progressed, Jay's join-in became louder and louder, until it, at times, harmonized with mine, and, at other times, actually drowned me out.

Together, we said: "Prophet!" said I, "thing of evil!—prophet still, if bird or devil! By that heaven that bends above us—by that God we both adore." Anyway, I thought that's what he was saying. Where my enunciation, to my credit, I thought, remained fairly clear and concise, his was getting downright guttural and only guess-if-it-was-right. "Tell this soul with sorrow laden if, within the distant Aidenn, It shall clasp a saintly maiden whom the angels name Lenore."

Suddenly, I needed a bit more concentration to make sure that everything stayed on an even keel, because his body, slotted to my body by my cock, was beginning to take on more animation than at the onset. Using his legs and arms as fulcrums, his torso swung back and forth, back and forth, to meet and retreat from every push and pull of my dick inside him. On his each backswing, his buttocks made a smacking sound as it contacted my lower belly, even with the muffling provided by my pubic hair and the hair that grew his ass like fur grew the butt of a monkey. The book became more and more likely to slip and slide if I didn't concentrate on keeping it in place, using the pressure of my thumbs. I began to find his continuing recitation of the poem, right along with me, as more than a little disconcerting, in that, more often than not, his were now merely undecipherable grunts, groans, and pretty much otherwise undecipherable guttural.

"And the lamp-light o'er him streaming throws his shadow on the floor; And my soul from out that shadow that lies floating on the floor...Shall be lifted— nevermore!" I finally competently completed, while Jay's sounds would likely have had Biblical folk, swearing that he spoke in tongues.

I was unsure what would happen next, not having had the forethought to ask beforehand if, once finished, I should just start over, or proceed reading the next poem— which, in this case, would have been *Lenore*.

My uncertainty, though, was only short-lived, because Jay was suddenly into full-blown orgasm, whinnying like a horse, and actually rearing up on his hind quarters, like a disturbed stallion, causing the book to slide, with a hard *thump*, into the wedge suddenly provided by his ass and my belly.

My arms parenthesized his midsection and contained him and the book. When he came on down, again, onto all fours, I curled over the top of him, my chin between his shoulder blades, the fingers of my hands interlocked under and across his stomach, my belly locked in tightly against his book and his ass.

I was so intent in my concentration, to keep everything as contained, that my orgasm came upon me almost totally unexpectedly, as did how my sudden squirts of cream into his bunghole seemed to reignite the previous intensity of his orgasm. Locked together, like two sex-linked rutting dogs, desperately in need of a dousing by ice-cold water, we rocked and rolled on that hotel-room floor, my spunk and his squirting every which way from Sunday, Poe and his poetry completely forgotten.

HAVEN

I met Haven Damer the summer after I graduated university. It was shortly after Klanze and Ross Publishing released the anthology *Ménage à Homo,* and the anthology surprisingly became a moderate best-seller, with even a couple of literary critics, apparently with their heads up their asses, jumping in to provide their high-brow interpretations of the deep-meanings inherent within my included novella, "Promiscuity 101", none of which ever crossed my mind, even vaguely, during my writing of it.

Haven came into his wealth late in life, the result of some long-forgotten aunt, on his mother's side, passing away in Romania. He had always had aspirations of becoming jaded, but had only recently gotten the money to make it happen; he was launched on a path that would allow him to experience all that he could, in the time he figured he had remaining—he had just turned seventy-five when I met him, his aunt having died but two years before.

He hadn't been fully accepted by society before he came into money, only reluctantly accepted afterwards; he held a genuine grudge against all the new friends his new money had bought him but who would automatically be bye-bye if ever his money went. He took to taking outsiders under his wing with whom he could purposely shock a lot of the hoity-toity "in" crowd.

"This is my friend, the pornographer," he invariably introduced me.

Maybe it was because *Ménage à Homo* really wasn't considered porn by readers or critics…or because I didn't look like a dirty old man…or because I did have a university degree…or because I could manage myself in polite society, even knew the difference between a finger bowl and a toilet bowl…that I was a less shocking specimen for Haven to pull out for display than, say, Garland Grill, freed of brutal rape and murder charges on a technicality, who was trotted out by Haven at one dinner party. More often than not, many of Haven's new friends were long-time friends of both Mr. Wins, and I found myself genuinely well-received and accepted as I tried to decide whether to take the job interviews already lined up for me in San Francisco, Los Angeles, and New York, at the beginning of the upcoming autumn, or, rather, to attempt writing the full-length book Jay kept insisting I "had" to write while the proverbial "iron" was hot. Of course, as it turned out, I canceled the former, and, it's only now that I'm finally finishing up the latter; all because Haven and I sat next to each other at a Save Venice Dinner. There had been another round of flooding in the art-rich Italian town, more of its (actually "the world's") masterpieces destroyed, others seriously water-damaged; grand dames of society, the world over, were, yet again, putting on fetes to raise cash to set right, or as right as possible, all the wrongs done Venice, yet again, by Mother Nature.

"You know," Haven said to me, seemingly as just another throwaway line of polite conversation, required by etiquette that ruled he should at least say something to each of us seated on either side of him during dinner, "I'm seriously considering hopping the next cruise ship around the world. We Americans are so damned puritanical, two-faced, back-stabbing, phony, and small-minded."

"Damned lucky you!" I said, spontaneously, and meant it. "That's something I've always wanted to do, too."

"Really?" he said. "Well, who knows, but that if you play your cards right, young man, you just might see it happen far sooner than you ever expected."

It was a conversation that might well have been cast aside as meaninglessly man-to-man flirtation by someone other than by me. In fact, even I might not have thought anything more of it if Parker Danep, somewhere later that same evening, hadn't queried, "Did you hear that old-man Damer is seriously soon to sail around the bloody world?" At which point, all of my instincts, inadvertently picked up and honed over the years, suddenly kicked into high gear.

While the royalties from *Ménage à Homo* had been divided three ways, between me and my two co-authors, and didn't, therefore, provide me nearly enough cash to sail around the world on my own, they did provide me enough to send Haven a dozen red roses. I figured he'd likely never had flowers sent to him; or, if he had, it had been a helluva along time since his last bouquet. I bought him a very expensive black cashmere sweater, too; not because he couldn't afford one, but because, despite his new wealth, I'd heard it bantered about that he was still miserly as regarded putting out real money for his wardrobe.

Six months later, my bank account only depleted by a couple thousand dollars, by way of gifts given to Haven, I boarded a luxury liner, first-class, headed around-the-world, with Haven footing the total bill and quickly taking to introducing me as his "nephew." The two Mr. Wins weren't particularly pleased, at first, having set up my job interviews with the ad agencies, only to have had to cancel them, but, each conceded, in the end, that being so hosted by the old man, even "this" old man—so old that no one, including me, ever dreamed he was still sexually active— was an opportunity I probably couldn't and shouldn't pass up. Gary saw why I was going, but wished I wasn't. Jay begrudgingly saw the advantages for life-experiences for me but insisted I take every opportunity to write while I was "on the high seas." My parents—especially my mother, who had always wanted to travel, but never had— were genuinely happy to see their son provided this unexpected opportunity to see the world.

Haven's choice of me, suddenly someone with a bit of cash of my own, as his traveling companion, had its pros and cons, as far as he was concerned. On the one hand, he would have been more assured of a favorable response to his eventual proposition for sex (wasn't I surprised to even hear it from someone his age?), if I were someone fully dependent upon his largesse; I told him I needed "to think on it." On the other hand, if and when I did say, yes, he had the psychological satisfaction, badly needed after his lifetime of feeling rejected, in knowing that it wasn't just his financial generosity that persuaded me to let him swing on my dick. Luckily for him, too, was my ability to get an erection, if necessary, for any old hole in any old stump … my ability to perform the sex act not really needing a genuine turn-on…and my ability to reason that it might be quite some time, should Haven decide to cut my trip short, before I had money enough of my own, or found another sugar daddy rich enough, to see me around the world (in other than the sexual connotation).

So, I came out of the shower, one evening, in one of the two owner's suites of our ship, which Haven and I were booked into for the duration, dropped my towel to reveal my stiffy behind it, and pretty much invited Haven to come on in ("Sueeee…Sueeee!"), to chow down. Nor did he need any second invitation. I don't think I've ever before, or ever since, seen a man, old or young, move as fast as he did, in his rush on over, in his kneel on down, in his grasp of my hard dick with one hand, in his cupping of the back of my right thigh for balance with his other hand, and in his immediate bow over, and swallow of, my cock, to begin some damned hearty eating.

"Easy, buddy," I instructed. Definitely, he seemed like a dog that hadn't eaten for days and was, now, afraid a newly found bone(r) was likely to be grabbed away from him before he'd finished with it. "I'm not going anywhere, and my cock isn't, either."

Soon, there was no doubt in my mind that Haven had spent a good deal of his earlier years down on his knees, doing what he was doing, and had retained a good deal of all that he'd learned while sucking however hundreds of cocks before he got to mine. He was good. He was damned good. Although, I couldn't help wondering if it would have been even better if he'd been one of the old folks who hadn't lucked out in keeping their own teeth (I'd later have someone blow me with both denture plates taken out, just for the sake of satiating my curiosity about just such a gumming—uniquely nice!).

I wasn't required by Haven to do much but stand there, so I didn't. I did put the fingertips of both hands to his shoulders (he was wearing a robe, in preparation for his own shower), and felt his skin and bone beneath the terry cloth. My hips began, eventually, a responsive to-and-fro sway that accompanied his sucking rhythm.

I did not shut my eyes and imagine that it was anyone but Haven going down on my hard prick...say, some genuinely studly young member of the ship's crew, like our dining-room waiter, Paolo. I've never been someone who needs any such fantasies, during sex, even when screwing inanimate objects, like the cushions of a couch. I'm far more interested in analyzing the specific pleasure to be had from fucking the sofa, or fucking Haven's face, than in trying to enhance it by imagining it something other than what it is. If Haven's suck of my prick didn't exactly have me climbing the walls with pleasure, no blowjob ever has. As long as the end result was my orgasm, and Haven showed no indication that he was prepared to stop before he achieved just that, I saw no reason, then, and I see no reason, now, ever to make something, including sex, anything other than what it is.

"Ohhhhh, that does feel good," I admitted. It's not like I'm ever completely excluded from at least some of those same pleasures likely experienced by others more excitable in such circumstances. It's just that my feeling good is definitely more contained than what I've witnessed in other men who can absolutely go ape-shit—screaming, shouting, moaning, groaning, gyrating—while their dicks fuck faces.

Automatically, my body responded to Haven's suck the way it responds to any suck. My cock got harder and drooled more pre-cum. My balls gathered up more and more compactly within my contracting scrotal bag that would eventually hug them to the base of my thick dick so tightly that they seemed disappeared.

There was tightness building within my lower belly.

"I'm going to come, buddy!" I provided warning. I've found it wise to provide warning. Even the most willing and eager cocksucker, working so damned hard for a draught of my cum, can actually be surprised by his success, maybe too tied up in the means to that end to realize when the end is upon him—or blasted into him. "If you're not ready, you'd better get that way."

Of course, Haven, with his mouth so chock full of my dick, couldn't do much more than emit guttural little sound-effects in response—which he did do. His lips clamped my dick harder. His fingers more forcefully squeezed the back of my leg.

"Here, I come," I promised, still giving him a few seconds more to prepare for the deluge which, even when conjured by the most inept cocksucker, is always impressive. "Here, I come. Here, I come. Here, I...agghgunnngummmm!"

His face took my first squirt on an upswing, my second squirt on a downswing. Both squirts were, then, swallowed, the resulting vacuum locking Haven's mouth down and around the base of my dick and holding it there, as my additional squirts, and his additional swallows, became quickly and skillfully synchronized so that he greedily sucked up all I had to offer him without losing a drop.

STAN

Our ship's on-board Emerald Spa came with the services of a masseuse and a masseur: Paula and Stan. Despite what a novice spa-goer might initially assume, the former wasn't exclusively for the women clientele, and the later wasn't exclusively for the men. The difference was that Paula delivered the kind of gentle massage some men and most women prefer. Stan's deep-muscle Rolfing was intense to the point of causing Mr. Landland, my fellow circle-the-world passenger and first-time spa-goer from Kansas (I was always tempted to ask if he knew my old university roomy, Theo, except Mr. Landland was into wholesale car parts; Theo, by then, was back forever into corn), to comment that Stan was definitely a sadist. Mr. Landland had quite enough of Stan and Rolfing, thank-you very much, and he had no intentions of trying any massage delivered by a woman, knowing as he did, from his Korean "give-you-a-special-massage-soldier-boy?" days, what happened when a woman got a man on a massage table; such shenanigans were okay in his sow-wild-oat days, but he was presently on a cruise with his wife; the couple had supposedly been happily married for over twenty-five years.

While I have no qualms whatsoever about turning over my body to a masseuse, and would have done so at the Emerald Spa, had Paula provided the kind of massage I preferred, it was Stan who I always booked; not because he was a man, and a decidedly very attractive blond, well-tanned, and muscled Scandinavian man, but because he really knew how to make me leave his table knowing that he'd gotten to, aligned, and loosened, each and every muscle in my admittedly fit-and trim-at-the-time body.

"There!" Stan said, providing a final deeply presented thumb print into the last-lingering bit of stiffness within my shoulder muscles along the very top of my back. "Roll over, if you would, please."

I continued shuddering, in direct response to the resulting pain/pleasure of his concluding back-rub punctuation by thumb, and said, as I usually did, well aware of the boner I sprouted, "You might want to give me a minute, or two, if you would, please."

After a brief and polite pause, he said, "You do know, and I've been meaning to tell you this, since day one, that a man getting aroused, during massage therapy is the rule, not the exception. I doubt seeing the physical evidence of your arousal is going to traumatize me for the rest of my life. I've been trained to deal with it, professionally...."—I was amusedly thinking of chiming in with, *By asking me if I'd like a special massage, solider?* but he finished with, "...by ignoring it completely."

I was curious to see where this would, or wouldn't go. Up until then...*even then*...Stan came off purely professional, no attempts at any probative double-entendre sexual repartee in his minimal conversation. What he'd just said was about as many words as I'd ever heard him string together at any one time. I thought about it for a moment and, then, obliged him by rolling to my back, careful to bring my towel along by way of suddenly obscene tenting over my swollen dick.

After which, there was nothing more said by either of us—except for my deep-muscle-alignment grunts and groans, until Stan's, "Finished," at massage conclusion, followed by his usual (get a record!) final-final, "but feel free to rest where you are for a few moments before you get dressed."

Was I disappointed that it hadn't progressed, between Stan and me, then and there, into something sexual? No. Admittedly, I was definitely drawn to him, as I was inevitably drawn to most attractive men, but certainly not to the point, with him, or with others, where I, like an animal in heat, felt it somehow imperative that sex between us happen, even if I had to do the seducing myself. I've met gay men so ruled by their cocks that their brains seem to check out completely, and I've always found them fascinating to observe, and a tad pathetic, in the way their testosterone, or whatever, compels them to chase after each and every man in pants as much as their heterosexual counterparts feel compelled to nail each and every woman in a skirt. Nor, as in the case of other gay men I've met, have I ever considered myself such a "dude magnet" that every man alive, gay or straight, is out to get in my pants (or, in the case of Stan, into my towel).

Truly, cross my heart, I was genuinely surprised, taken back, even shocked, when several weeks later, after what, by then, had become just another automatic I-am-dealing-with-a-professional-here rollover by me to my back on the message table, boner intact, Stan said, "I really hope you and Mr. Damer aren't really uncle and nephew."

"Beg your pardon?" That's exactly what I said, unable to think of anything else.

"I'd hate to think your big cock is going to complete waste, except for you beating it, nightly, or just using it to piss," he kept right on going, where up until then, I had thought him possibly foreign (Norwegian? Swedish?) and a tad inept with his grasp of the English language. "From what I've seen and heard, you're certainly not sharing it with crew or passengers, male or female, even though more than a few have made it perfectly clear that they're available."

"You're kidding, right?" Obviously, if anyone, at the moment, was suffering from ineptness with the English language, it was I.

"I get to ask, because my father is ill," he said; certainly, I didn't get where there was any connection between the two. "As soon as we dock in Singapore, first of next week, I have to fly home to be with him, and, up until now, I've been too much the professional to ask you questions and risk you turning me in and getting me fired for making a homo-pass at you."

Suddenly, I felt very vulnerable laid out on his table; he was a strapping young man whose massage training, and obvious gym workouts, put him in genuinely fine physical shape. Granted, I had a few martial art lessons under my belt, but still....

"You really still don't have a clue, do you," he continued, "as to just how hot and horny I get, every time I give you a massage, to the point where I have to go off somewhere and jack off before my next customer?"

Okay, imagining that happening, which I still wasn't sure was the truth (fleetingly, I wondered if this was some kind of test or practical joke Haven was pulling), actually got me a tad more excited than usual.

"Well, certainly, I have a clue, now, don't I?" I said. "Color me flattered."

"Meaning, it's true you're gay; Mr. Damer just refuses to share you?"

"Meaning, it's never really come up for discussion—yet."

"You're the one who's kidding, now, right?"

"While Haven is, admittedly, paying most of my bills..."

"Ah-ha," he interrupted, "I thought so!"

"...he's never really said I couldn't find an occasional bit of fun and games on the side; I've just never been so inclined—until now." I'd added the codicil, because I was suddenly, admittedly, very seriously interested as to how Stan looked when stripped entirely down to nothing but his exceptionally tanned, exceptionally blond, exceptionally studly, exceptionally Scandinavian muscles and bare skin.

"Surely, you've been tempted, at last once, by someone on board." He didn't sound as if he was in the least convinced by my statement to the contrary.

"Before now, you mean? No, I've never been tempted."

"Are you tempted, now? Really? Or, are you just making fun and leading me on?"

"I'm very desirous of seeing you stark naked. Think there's any chance that might happen?"

"First…." He took hold of my towel and pulled it free of my lower body. My hard cock made its official appearance, and stayed hard, despite the cool breeze the whipped-towel had provided in parting.

"Jesus Christ!" he said. "Do you know how long I've been hoping to get a genuinely prolonged look at this cock of yours? I even tried, more than once, to spot you in the spa shower—damn those private stalls."

"Having seen myself naked plenty of times," I said, "I'm actually hoping to see you this way—soon."

Rather than commence the quick and hurried strip for which I hoped—how long, after all, would it take him to shed his pull-over knit shirt, white chinos, and tennis shoes (no socks)?—he said, "Can I touch it?"

"Why don't you get undressed, first?" I suggested, for not the first time.

He touched my bare right leg, raising goose bumps. His hand, far more gently than ever in deep-massage, ran up and along the inside of my right thigh, as far as my hairy nuts.

My cock jerked where it was laid out against my six-pack abs; it oozed pre-cum from its eye that left a sticky pool as pillowing for its pulpy head.

"Shit!" he said, took immediate hold of my dick, lifted it so it pointed toward the ceiling, and started pumping it like there was no tomorrow.

I was going to complain that turnabout was fair play but was assuaged, if only somewhat, by how his left hand started fumbling at his pants crotch and soon—his massage training over the years having obviously made him ambidextrous, if he hadn't been born that way—had his fly quickly and skillfully open. If he'd have only slowed down the speed and forcefulness with which he beat my meat, my eyes not too quickly blurred with my swelling passion, I was convinced there was a good chance I'd soon see his naked cock, if not the naked rest of him.

Success! And what a marvelous dick his is, too, being just as strapping, and as big-boy impressive, as the rest of his accompanying stud-muffin anatomy His thick foreskin immediately was tugged and pushed to cover and uncover his cock's bulbous corona, albeit at a decidedly slower rhythm than his other hand continued to whip the quickly priming length of my hard dick.

None of it, once begun, lasted all that long. The swiftness of his beating our dicks to pretty much simultaneous cum blasts was the direct result of his frantic efforts spawned, I'd learn later, by his utter frustration in having for so long having wanted my cock, so long having been in close proximity to it, but having so long been kept from it—if just by his own professional self-restraint. Once he actually saw my naked cock, he said later, he almost spontaneously creamed his chinos. Once he had his hand actually wrapping my erection, he thought for sure there was no way on God's blue sea that he'd ever get his cock out of his pants before ejaculating, let alone ever see his fast-approaching-orgasm actually coincide with mine.

By some miracle, though—don't ask me how, unless it was my unusual degree of turn-on caused by all the spontaneity which isn't usually present when I have sex—as soon as his cock squirted its great gobs of pearly cream against the side of the massage table and hot lattice-splattered all over my right side, my prick erupted full-force, looking every bit like Old Faithful letting go magma-heated geyser spray.

Later, Stan told me to book as many massages from him as I wanted, between then and his departure from the ship at Singapore, because all of them would be on the house.

When Haven began to guess what was up at the Emerald Spa (my cock and Stan's), I merely commented, in passing, that "my masseur" was leaving the ship at Singapore—at the same time, I pulled down my pants for Haven's head to have another bounce over it—and Haven never made any kind of a fuss.

TREVOR

Originality is hard to come by. How many times have I read a book, seen a movie, watched a TV show, and said to myself, or to whomever was with me, at the time, "I've seen this all before"? That's exactly why people with true ingenuity and creativity often get paid big bucks. In a world become increasingly more and more jaded, with each and every passing day, it's damned hard to achieve the high of NOT having been there, done that, gotten the T-shirt.

Therefore, it probably shouldn't have come as any big surprise, and didn't, when, while the ship was docked in Hong Kong, another "uncle" and "nephew" duo, Trevor Dean and Merlin Paynes, joined Uncle Haven and Nephew Me on the passenger list.

It's wrong to assume that anyone on a round-the-world cruise is hobnobbing entirely with vacationers who are doing one and the same thing, even when sailing on the very same ship. Our exclusive little group of "worldies", an exact dozen, was a decided minority, at any one time. Mainly, we could be thought of as a kind of permanent "insider" clique in a school that continually had its influx and outflow of transient students. Our little, "in" group, scheduled to be on board for the ship's entire circumvention of the globe, and, thus, better known by the staff and crew, better knowing them, did tend to cluster, as during regular dinners at the captain's table, or off to ourselves for private member-only banquets and member-only cocktail parties. On the whole, though, the passenger roster always consisted more of people, like Trevor and Merlin, who booked for shorter junkets—in their case Hong Kong to Bali—and it was hard for us "worldies" to avoid them; even if we'd wanted to, which definitely wasn't the case as soon as Haven and I realized, as did likely everyone else who wanted to give it a second's thought, that Trevor and Merlin were two more gay guys providing the uncle-nephew "beard" as their way of best fitting in.

Haven genuinely bonded with Trevor who, though a self-made man, had, like Haven, known years of not exactly being held in high esteem by polite society. Trevor had recently sold his construction company and had decided to have some of the fun and games denied him in his prime. Likely a good twenty years Haven's junior, he was a short stocky man, with thick black hair, black eyes, black and bushy eyebrows, bulbous nose, thin lips, and skin that looked not only baked-way-too-brown in the sun but was cracked and lined like the exposed bone-dry silt of some long-evaporated river bed. His clothes, if expensive, didn't look expensive, in that he really didn't possess the body or demeanor to show them off properly; if doing so doesn't always require a long and lean silhouette, although that helps, it does require certain panache to make them seem as if they belong to the wearer, instead, as in Trevor's case, just the opposite. Also, his dress shoes were never polished, and his canvas deck shoes were always too crisp and clean. None of which would have automatically made me dislike him, except that all of that was accompanied by his disconcerting rude and disrespectful treatment of his younger traveling companion to the point of making it definitely clear, by words and actions, that Merlin wouldn't have had a pot to pee in if Trevor ever decided to stop providing it.

Admittedly, Merlin wasn't the sharpest tack in the corkboard, thereby hardly living up to his namesake. He came off painfully shy; at times, to the point of actually shirking. However, whenever coaxed into conversation, he was always polite and respectful, if decidedly soft-spoken. He had light-brown hair, light-brown eyes, snub nose, nice lips, a very small cleft in his chin, and a body so waif-like that I was tempted, more than once, to comment that Trevor might think of buying the kid something to eat, except that there was an overabundance of free food on board—in fact literally tons of it—each and every hour, of each and every day, and of each and every night.

"What would you say to my fucking Merlin?" Haven surprised me by asking, one morning, just after breakfast, as I was preparing to go out on deck for some tanning rays, and he was preparing for his by-then-regular rounds of bridge played in one of the ship's lounges until lunch time. "I mean, you really wouldn't care, would you?"

I hardly had room to complain, even if I'd wanted, considering how decent he'd been about my marathon fucking around with Stan up until we'd docked in Singapore.

"Go for it, buddy," I said, "but don't you really think you should be asking Trevor, instead of me?"

"Actually, Trevor suggested it."

"Really?"

"He said I could have Merlin whenever I wanted him, because Trevor was the one who said what and who Merlin did, or didn't, do."

"Sounds just like something Trevor would say."

"He did provide a caveat."

"Such a big word you have, there, Uncle dear."

"It merely means…."

"I know what it means, Haven. Just get on with your story."

"He'd like me to reciprocate…."

"Such another big word you have, there, Unc."

"…by sharing you."

"Would he now?" I had a hard time believing Trevor's interest in me was real, unless he knew I didn't particularly like him, and he got off by forcing himself on people who would like to say no but had little choice in the matter.

"I said I'd ask you," Haven confessed.

"Which must have had Trevor wondering what in the holy hell is up with the two of us. His never having to ask Merlin's input on anything, I can just imagine why he thought I shouldn't have any say in the matter, either? What a genuine shit that man is."

"Some people, I hear, get turned on by shit."

"One of whom has to be Merlin, right, for the kid to have stuck around this long with that stinky old turd?"

"Right." Haven sounded unconvinced and downright crestfallen.

"You would, however, really like to fuck Merlin, wouldn't you?" Hell, I could easily conclude that, just by listening to, and looking at, him. "I mean you are like really, really hot to have at that kid's skinny little ass, aren't you?"

"He's cute, and Trevor says the kid is a lot less inhibited in bed than anyone might think upon meeting him."

So, was it my day to play Good Samaritan, taking into account that Stan and I had fucked up a storm, and Haven hadn't raised any kind of fuss or rumpus? I mean, it wasn't exactly as if I couldn't get a boner and perform with men I didn't particular like or find attractive, although shit-head Trevor just might be the exception.

"Let me think about it," I decided, because I really didn't like Trevor; I really didn't find him in the least attractive.

Haven had the goodness-graciousness to let it go at that. It was actually Trevor, later that same day, who checked in next on the matter, sliding over an adjoining deck chair so that it physically abutted mine, sitting down in it and making its slates creak, pulling his aviator sunglasses down the bridge of his bulbous nose to better see me over them, and saying, "What're you reading?"

I turned my open copy of *Anna Karenina* in his direction.

"Don't mean to spoil it for you, but the bitch dies in the end," he said and smiled. Some people have smiles that radiate their faces and make them genuinely handsome, even if they aren't handsome before smiling.

Trevor's smile didn't work that magic; he remained as un-attractive as ever.

"So how much did you pay someone to read the book and pass on that bit of information?"

He laughed, which did even less for him that his lead-in smile had.

"I like you, kid," he said, "which is why I'd so much like to fuck you."

"I'm considering the sex," I said, "although I was sure Haven said it would be you stuck on the end of my stiff dick."

Rather than go into his he-man-who-never-had-his-ass-fucked-and-never-would routine, which I expected, he just pursed his lips and said, "You really think you're man enough to screw me?"

"You seem to think you're man enough to fuck Merlin; you see any big difference?"

"You just may be surprised to discover me a tad more versatile in the bedroom than Merlin is, if I'm ever there with the right person. How is either of us to know if you're that right person, though, if you don't give it a go?"

"I didn't say I wouldn't. What I did say was that I would think about it. Who knows but that you might luck out? Sometimes even double 0 comes up a winner in rou-lette."

He pushed his glasses back along the broad ridge of his nose to make his black eyes look even more bug-like. He laid full-out in the deck chair and, simultaneously, pulled his Yankee baseball cap down more tightly over his head. He called out to a passing steward, "Hey kid, bring me double bourbon on the rocks, and refill my friend's glass, here."

The steward was gone with our orders before I could stop him. Not that I would have stopped him. Yes, please, and thank-you, was more and more becoming my mantra, especially when there was, at least as of yet, no strings attached.

"Haven tells me you have a bit of money of your own," he said. "Wrote some kind of book, which I looked for in the ship's library but couldn't find."

"Go figure." I said.

"Merlin doesn't have any money of his own," he said, "in case you haven't been able to tell."

"Certainly, I already guessed that had to be the only reason he was with you."

"You don't think he hangs around with me because of my charm?"

"Jesus, no!"

He laughed. If nothing else, he impressed me by the easy way he managed to accept my insults."

"Merlin is Merlin," he said. "You are you. You're both of interest to me, not the least because the two of you seem to be the only passengers on board this ship who are this side of senility."

"There's always the captain and the crew."

"I never have been one to fuck the help. So, how about if I paid you a little on the side?"

"Didn't you just tell me that Haven told you that I have money of my own?"

"Doesn't everyone, except, maybe, Merlin?" he said, with an accompanying very wide smile that showed teeth regular enough but definitely in need of some serious whitening. "The real question, of course, is: Does anyone, even you, ever really have nearly enough money?"

So, while I ended up naked in his cabin, his having paid me cash, up front, after he made a special trip to the purser's office, I would likely have ended up there on any account. I'd come genuinely to like Haven, and I figured he deserved a little goodie, now and then. Besides which, Trevor was one more male specimen to be observed, up close and personal.

In truth, he looked far better out of his clothes than in them. Obviously, his years in construction work hadn't all been spent behind a desk. His muscles were beginning to fat over, but they were still honed-in-the-field evident, here, there, and pretty much everywhere—arms, chest, belly, back, and legs. Rather than being tremendously hirsute, as I'd expected, he had just the right amount of hair to highlight perfectly, rather than conceal, his musculature—the roundness of his pecs and the run of deep cleavage that divided them, the ridges of his stomach, the small and not unattractive knotting of his navel, and the curves and crack of his ass. Even his pubic bush was low-grown (frequently scissor-trimmed by him?), and provided just enough parentheses of his cock and balls to make them stand-out. Granted, his wasn't the biggest cock I've ever seen, probably made less impressive by its sloppy circumcision...nor were his balls exactly bull-like...but neither his cock nor his balls had anything to fear from any comparisons with other sexual equipment found in the world's locker rooms.

While I was taking him in, he was doing the same of me. Although he'd already had more than one peek at me swimming in the pool and sunning on deck, I'd yet to see him stripped down as completely as he was, then and there.

"Definitely, you're more of a man than Merlin could ever think to be," he said. "Shall we have a bit of wrestling to determine who fucks who?"

His downfall, of course, as it is with so many men who have probably been bullies all of their lives, and have had the body bulk to back it up, is that, after years and years of succeeding at what they do so well, they become overconfident. Granted, I came to the party pretty well-muscled, but it still must have looked to him, as it did to me, as if I was merely a well-conditioned swimmer suddenly confronted by an athlete Olympic-medaled for power-lifting. Just because he outweighed me, though, didn't mean that he could best me, and my martial-arts know-how, in any fight, or, as it turned out, in any pretty one-sided tussle that damned quickly put his muscled chest and belly to the bed, me riding his ass and back, and my un-lubricated cock socked so hard and fast up his asshole that he actually grunted like a stuck pig as, and after, he took it.

In fact, he turned out to be one of those big bullies who exemplify that often heard bit of usually just wishful thinking: *Ah, I'll bet he really just wants to find someone butch enough to stick hard cock up his tight man-pussy ass and make him dance like a puppet on a stick.* Once I had him pinned…my dick not only deep inside his asshole but working there with all the expertise I'd learned during all my years of fucking…the struggle went all out of Mr.

Tough Guy, and he became like putty to be played with and manipulated. In no time, I had him moaning, groaning, whimpering, simpering, and begging me to, "Stick that manly monster cock…deeper, deeper! Screw! Screw! Baby, yes. Screw! Oh, yes! Fuck your daddy's tight asshole! Shit-pack daddy's shit with your pile-driver…dick!" (He's a poet; he doesn't know it; his feet show it: they're long-fellows).

I grabbed a handful of his thick black hair and gave it the tug necessary to pull his face up from where it was buried and moaning in the bedspread. His arched neck put his large Adam's apple into high relief. My mouth went to the side of his neck and, in a vampire kiss, bit down hard.

His resulting orgasm was so violent that it literally did more toward dislodging me from him than all of his struggles prior to, and during, my fuck of him. He accompanied with loud bullish huffs and puffs reminiscent of *el torro* I'd once heard panting, fully exhausted, in the Madrid bullring, after several grueling and successful passes by a very famous matador.

Certainly, it was a good enough ride for me to join on in, at the finale, with a bit of hearty cum-squirting of my own. I can definitely say that I basted his bully tight asshole royally.

JOHN

"I'm Jay's assistant, John McBurney," he said, took my hand in his and shook it.

He has a firm grip. He has reddish blond hair. While I'm usually not particularly fond of redheads, he's an exception to the rule. Maybe it's because his complexion is pleasingly tanned, not pasty-white (or pasty-white-burned-lobster-red). He surprised me by having black eyes, instead of the expected green, grey, or blue. He looked genuinely good in his Draqual black matte-silk sports coat and Draqual charcoal-colored slacks. His button-down dark-blue Oxford shirt had its collar button open to reveal an attractive vee of hairless tanned skin. He body is trim but not skinny.

"What happened to Sheila?" I asked; Sheila had been Jay's assistant.

"She got preggies. Color Jay livid. Not that Jay was the father." He smiled as if we had just shared the very same insider joke; which we had. "He swears he'll never hire another fertile cunt. Certainly, he avoided that by hiring me." He provided another intimate smile to be shared by just the two of us. "By the way, his plane has been socked in by bad weather at Orly. Definitely, he'll be flying in from Paris tomorrow and sends his regards and con-dolences until then. In the meantime, per his instructions, I've pretty much completed all the arrangements for the eventual forwarding on of you and the coffin of your friend. I suggest we now get you squared away with cus-toms, here, and settled into your hotel room where you can freshen up and rest a bit."

"Seems strange to freshen up and rest a bit, just re-turned from a vacation."

"It couldn't have been easy for you, having Mr. Damer die on you."

I only thanked the dear God that Haven hadn't "liter-ally" died "on" me by having his heart failure while he was sucking my cock and, somehow, in the midst of his death throes, simultaneously drowning on my cum, or, worse, biting off my penis. Haven had the goodness-graciousness to die in his sleep, during an afternoon siesta, while I was out on deck, reading the last of *War and Peace,* drinking chilled Veuve Clicquot, and eating Xoçai chocolate. He'd, likewise, obliged me by waiting to die until we were on the last leg of our round-the-world. Fi-nally, most goodness-gracious, endearing, and surprising, of all, he'd had the paperwork drawn up, signed, and le-gally witnessed, on board ship, two weeks before he died, to make me his official heir and, except for some minor charitable contributions, his chief beneficiary.

Jay had booked me into the thirty-seventh-floor pent-house suite at the Fontainebleau; I hadn't a clue what I was supposed to do with the two extra bedrooms; since, he was footing the bill, I didn't much care, either. Over ship-to-shore, he had been insistent that we talk before I fly off into the wild-blue yonder with Haven's remains and my newly acquired fortune.

"Do you mind if you and I talk for a few minutes, now, or would you rather I come back later," John asked as soon as the bellboy had shown us in, been tipped by John, and sent on his way.

"Now's fine," I said. Actually, I wasn't feeling all that bad. I'd had several days on the high seas to get over the unexpectedness of Haven passing; although, why I found it unexpected that man his age should suddenly drop dead, I haven't a clue. Checking through Port of Miami customs, on the north side of Dodge Island, had gone smoother than I'd expected. All arrangements, as regarded the coffin transfer, and my accompaniment, had been efficiently taken care of by John; I'd be flying Haven back to some long-time family cemetery in Nevada of all places. The Fontainebleau suite accommodations were first-rate, including its well-stocked wet bar. "Would you like a drink?"

"Whatever you're having, please," John said and took a seat while I poured us both a couple fingers of Draqual vodka on the rocks.

I joined him, handed over his drink, took the chair opposite, sipped my vodka, and waited.

"Jay still wants that promised book, for sure," John said. "Of course, now he's afraid, since you're rolling in inherited money, that you might not feel any need to be creative. I'm supposed to remind you, before he checks in to reinforce what I say, that the idle rich grow quickly bored, drunken, and even suicidal."

"My God, how considerate of you, both, to want to bring that to my attention."

"Jay told me you began a book while on your cruise."

I did remember having told Jay just that when speaking to him on the phone from somewhere along the way. It was pretty much a patent exaggeration, though. I was never convinced by his continual assurances that my first literary effort, successful as it admittedly had been, still had any publisher actually interested in anything I could come up with by way of follow-up.

"I merely jotted down some notes about my travels," I confessed. No reason to pretend otherwise. Had I been hot to replenish cash-depleted coffers, and/or genuinely out to achieve literary stardom, it would have been another matter; but, as things stood.... "I'm thinking, maybe, of just holing up on some tropical island for awhile and mourning poor Haven's passing."

John paid absolutely no attention to that suggestion, and said, "Jay knows exactly what he wants from you, this time around. He sent me to pitch the idea; not because he doesn't think you deserve the star treatment of having him pitch it personally...not just because he's presently socked in by the weather at Orly...but because he thinks you might appreciate something arrived on your doorstep a tad more different than the same old guy, with the same old book of Poe poetry, wanting you to do the same old thing, yet again, especially since you've already been that route."

"I was wondering if there was a volume of poetry concealed within your document bag."

"Actually, I arrive with no poetry, only my ability to wrap my feet and ankles around my neck and suck my cock while you fuck my asshole."

"Okay, that certainly has my interest, "I admitted. No shit, Sherlock! As usual, my curiosity had me more fascinated by the unique human-contortionist aspects of his offer than by his invite for sex. I'd never fucked someone who had his feet and ankles locked around his neck while eating his own cock.

"Jay wants you to write a book about male hustling; something mainly upbeat, with lots and lots of graphic sex. Something about how some guys make a fortune in that profession, selling their bodies. He already has a publisher chomping at the bit to have at it."

"Not exactly my area of expertise, like college sex once was."

"Huh?" He sounded all you-have-to-be-joking. "Are you not just back from a world cruise where you played nephew and returned a very rich young man?"

"Jay wants me to write myself as a male hustler who made it big?" I had to admit, it could well look that way to some people, but….

"As good looking as you are, he's confident that you likely have a whole series of money-for-sex encounters in your past, from which you can draw roman-a-clef inspiration, culminating with this last little world-cruise business deal of Haven and yours that certainly rockets you into the Hustlers' Hall of Fame; all with potential for one fantastic best-selling read."

"Granted, I've had some such experiences, but I doubt they're nearly enough to fill a whole book."

"We figured if that was the case, you could supplement with input from several other hustlers with success stories similar to your own."

"These similar hustler success stories found just where, exactly?"

"I know someone whose name I can give you. Jay says he knows someone who knows someone who can get you another name. Do you doubt that you have the charm, expertise, know-how, and, now, the money, to track down a few others on your own; at least enough to give you your needed word count?"

"Do I really want to come across to the world as a male prostitute, even one who made it into the big time?"

"You know that's what people are thinking, anyway, don't you? If you're going to get the blame, you might as well get the fame."

"Did you just coin that rhyme off the top of your head? And, please, tell me you don't expect me to repeat it, by rote, while I'm fucking you."

He laughed. "Well, it was off the top of my head, all right, but I think someone else thought it up before I did, just don't ask me who. Okay, not exactly off the top of my head, either, in that I planned to use it all along. However, I'll not require you to repeat it and fuck me at one and the same time. I'm only hoping you'll let me strip down, here and now, lock my ankles and feet around my neck, my mouth around my dick, while your cock does fuck me."

"After which, you do know—if I do put my signature on the dotted line—that you'll likely end up a chapter in my new book? Any such chapter not only illustrating how I'm still pimping my body for payment, this time for a book contract, but doing so with a hustler, with potential for the big time, who's pimping his body to see my signature put there."

"I'm already so far out of the closet that I'd only be flattered to be included."

"Maybe, I should really have a bit more time to think about this." I finished my drink and made the remaining ice *clink* against the sides of the containing lead crystal.

"Except, wouldn't I come off more a success in hustling—for the purpose of your book, I mean—if I actually got the contract signed, sealed, and delivered, on my own, not needing Jay to arrive to finalize?"

"Do you even have the contract drawn up?"

He patted the document bag that was, all of this time, hung by its strap over his left shoulder (containing contract, not Poe poetry?).

"I admit that I'd like, at the very least, to see you naked, ankles and feet locked behind your neck, dick sucked into your face." I put my empty-except-for-ice glass on the end table next to my chair. The fingers of both my hands made a contemplative tepee beneath my chin.

"I could do it for you, right over there, on the dining-room table," he said. The suite has kitchen facilities. Its heavy-duty table and chairs easily seat eight. "Once my position is assumed, you can pull me even closer to the edge, and my asshole will be pretty much perfectly aligned for taking in your dick once you've pulled your cock out of your pants; or, even better, just dropped your pants; even best, gotten stark naked by discarding your pants entirely."

I adjusted the way my stiff dick was situated in my trousers. Its swelling had put it into a cul-de-sac of folded material that didn't allow it full expansion.

"Hey, what do you think of the coincidence that has me with one of those, too?" John said and outlined the exceedingly large stiffness of his cock, as if it needed additional emphasis, laid out against his left thigh.

"I will say that I'm glad neither of us is seriously considering my taking that monster of yours up my asshole," I said.

"We are, then, yes, please, considering your dick up mine?" He put his empty-except-for-ice glass onto his chair's side table. He stood. He started to undress.

I watched him for a few seconds, and, then, stood to join him. His emerging body looked as if it, not mine, was the one out to sea for lengthy lounging in beneficent sunshine; it was toasty brown and looked just like rippled tan silk, especially his washboard belly. He had hard dark pink nipples, dime-size; his innie bellybutton held no lint.

I was unbuttoning my shirt, when he dropped his pants. I stopped what I was doing to marvel at the now-even-more definitive outline of his cock and balls, in just his gray briefs, without any interference from trouser material. There was a large swollen mass at the very bottom-center of his underpants from which sprouted an obviously long thick tube that jutted upward, at an angle, to termination at the waistband of his hugging shorts, very near his left hipbone. Where the elongation ended, there was a big-as-a-poker-chip pre-cum wet spot.

He hooked his thumbs into the elastic of the waistband and pulled out from his midsection. This released the tilt of his dick and allowed his cock to achieve full-attention; its head projected upward in front of his muscled belly well beyond his navel.

While I continued to watch, fascinated, he slid his shorts down his hips, along his flanks, and over his ass; at the same time, the sloughing material revealed the entire naked length of his huge dick, and his voluptuous cascading scrotum that hung his monster balls in perfect accompaniment. When his hands released all contact with his underpants, the weight of the material gravity-dropped them to his feet.

He stepped out of his clothes, out of his shoes, and said, "You don't mind if I pause, here and now, to watch you finish undressing, do you?"

I obliged, although it was one of the few times in my life when I thought my cock, sizable as it was, didn't stand up well in comparison with the other cock in the room. Certainly, though, John, either diplomat, or hustler out for my signature on the contract, didn't say as much. Quite to the contrary, he said, "Very, very, very nice, from the top of your head, to the tip of your toes, including each and every thing in between." It would have been a perfect opportunity for him to have said, "...every 'little' thing in between." At least, my dick had a good chance of deeply drilling his asshole, without the risk of tearing him from stem to stern—which couldn't have been said of his dick had it been scheduled to make a run up my rectum.

"Okay, then," he said and headed for the leading edge of the table; I followed after him. He turned toward me in order to back his naked ass into position. He placed the palms of both hands flat on the table's highly polished wooden surface, and he hoisted himself into a leg-dangling sit. "You might want to step on up to give me an assist, at this point, just in case I need one. I won't be nearly as enjoyable a fuck if I've fallen on the floor and been knocked unconscious as a result."

I stepped on in, my hard cock not only leading the way but weeping a pre-cum tear in joy at the prospect of the unusual fuck being held out for it.

We were suddenly so close, I between his open thighs, that our balls actually touched and tickled, our sac hair intermingling. Had his cock and mine been held a little less tightly, by stiffness, into snug alignments against our stomachs, our cock bellies would have touched for sure.

"Hmmmmm," he said and put one hand to each of my upper arms, "nothing like two fit and trim studly young men about to get it on."

Without any help needed, his right leg rose along my left side, and his foot and ankle, easy as you please, assumed a position behind his head.

"Jesus!" I marveled. "Doesn't that hurt?"

"The secret is in maintaining the exercise regimen that keeps me limber," he said and lifted his other leg. This time, though, he used his left hand to maneuver his left foot and ankle in order to lock them with his other foot and ankle. His body tilted slightly back, and his balls left my balls to slide upward as far as the base of my stiff dick.

"And, there you have it," he said, without sounding in the least boastful; I suspect if I had been able to achieve such a feat, I would have come off far more exceedingly nah-nah-nah-nah…nah-nah.

I would have liked stepping back for a better look, but, frankly, I was afraid he would teeter on the edge and topple on over, or roll, like a tire, off to one side, or to the other, before I could get back to him, or before he could come un-pretzeled.

"Do you think we two hustlers are only one fuck away from sealing our deal?" he asked. A lock of his strawberry hair fell onto his forehead, and he managed to do very little but temporarily shift it by trying to blow it back into place. Since he, again, held firmly to me with both hands, I felt it safe enough to use my right hand to reposition his attractively recalcitrant strands back to from where they'd fallen.

"Now, if you could just put your cock up my ass, please," he said.

Actually, the table wasn't perfectly aligned for my cock to achieve the most opportune access to John's asshole, in that the tabletop was just a tad too low. I was required to bend both of my legs, slightly at my knees, to bring my balls down to a complete pooling on the cool surface of the highly polished wood; my hips swung back, and my right hand pressured my stiff dick from its position parallel to my body to one that protruded it from me like a draw-bridge. I slotted my pulpy cock head into the pink-winked eye of his closed sphincter.

His body rocked, slightly, left and right, leaving sweat marks on the tabletop to either side of him. My hips began the push that quickly put my cock head to complete disappearance within his small and tight anal opening that punctuated the crack of his ass.

His cock, stiff between his belly and mine, jerked and leaked pre-cum that overflowed and smeared a large pie-slice section of cock head, all of the way to the edge of its coronal flare. His balls moved within his compacting scrotum and rolled the latter's strawberry blond hair like a forest fire on the move.

My cock no longer needed any help in keeping it from springing back into full-obelisk position; so, my hands slid John's waist and, then, dropped farther to cup his buttocks. They held firmly, there, while my hips continued their swing toward the tabletop and toward John atop it. My cock seemed more and more foreshortened as it progressed into more and more disappearance up John's accepting body. Until finally, I didn't seem to have my dick at all, merely the growth that was John's contorted body, complete with John's impressive dick, attached directly to the base of my belly.

"Ohhhh, that feels so fucking good," he said, his ass again rocking from side to side on the tabletop and providing more and more polish to the already shiny wood.

It was strange being up so close and personal to his face and smelling not only the peppermint mint he'd obviously, somehow, managed to suck after his drink and before his sitting the table but, also, the slight funkiness of his feet.

I rested my right cheek against his right cheek, my forehead actually resting against the heel of one foot. Momentarily, I thought about sucking his toes while I fucked him, but a sudden contraction of his anus, squeezing the total length of my prick deep inside of him, diverted my attention to down the front of his torso and mine to where my lower belly smashed in so tightly against the widened crack of his ass. In between us, his dick, looking bigger than ever, seemed a rocket about to be launched, fuel drooling its nozzle-like head.

His hands held tightly to me. My hands held tightly to him.

I commenced the pushes and pulls that sent my dick into constant and more pronounced movement within him.

He rocked some more. He rolled some more.

I shoved my dick all of the way home; his asshole went concave with each insertion of my cock. I pulled my dick out until only my cock head slotted his butt; his asshole went convex with each withdrawal of my stiff and fucking boner from, and through, it.

My balls dragged the tabletop, heated by the resulting friction and leaving a sweaty smear that matched those made by the roll of his butt on the wooden surface. My scrotum became more and more tightly gathered to the base of my ass-fucking dick. Looking down at my nuts, I saw just how tightly their sac had them vacuum packed and totally confined; they looked like a single basketball.

I was very glad John was there. I was very glad that he'd sat the table, wrapped and locked his feet and ankles around his neck. I was glad he'd invited my dick to stick deep up has asshole. I was glad I'd taken him up on his offer.

If his doing what he was doing, and my doing what I was doing, actually committed me to writing a book for Jay, I was more than content with that bargain made. God only knew when the next opportunity would present itself for me to fuck under such unique circumstances. God only knew that I probably did need something to do to keep me occupied, besides just spending the money Haven left me.

I was having such a thoroughly unique and interesting time of it that I would have possibly even forgotten, until sometime after my nuts busted, that there had been more promised me than just what was, then, ongoing. John, probably more often in similar situations, and, therefore, less distracted and more able to concentrate, luckily remembered for the both of us.

"If I'm going to eat my dick, you might want to pull your cock almost out, at least for a moment or two, and hold on to me to make sure I don't get overbalanced," he whispered into my ear; the thought of his actually sucking his dick, as well as being tied all up in a knot, my cock screwed up his rectum, almost saw me creaming right then and there. If I'd been anyone else, in a similar situation, I'd bet good money that my nuts would have popped, nothing more needed. Curiosity, though, for not the first time in my life, overrode pure passion, and saw me determined not to miss any part of the performance John had promised as part of our deal.

My dick pulled out to where John's pursed sphincter gummed my cock head just beneath the impressive flare of my cock's corona. I pulled my face away from his face and away from his locked-behind-his-neck feet and ankles to provide more space between us.

His head bowed, its top suddenly pressed into my chest, and slid downward, as John's upper torso went into the tight curl that I suspected would quickly have his open mouth within striking distance of his stiff penis.

Still holding to his ass, I leaned back so that my arms, as well as his, were fully extended. Therefore, I saw the exact moment his mouth set down atop his pre-cum juiced cock head and slid right on over it to make it disappear.

"Sweet Jesus!" I complimented his exceptional dexterity.

My cock twitched so violently that I thought it might actually dislodge itself from the headlock John's sphincter had on it. Automatically, my hips returned another inch of my dick into John's asshole, as John's face sucked up another inch of his dick. I fucked John another inch of my hard cock; he swallowed another hard inch of his.

I've since learned that he can self-eat his cock all of the way to his balls, but he didn't that day. Not because he wasn't up to the pleasurable task of duplicating what he'd done many times before, but because even jaded old me had finally been subjected to enough visual and physical stimuli to erupt into full-blown orgasm.

My cock slammed all of the way up his butt and stayed there. My hands clamped super tightly against his ass cheeks. My ass cheeks deeply dimpled.

I shot more and more of my wads.

Simultaneous with my pearly spunk basting the deep insides of his guts, John's head popped free of his erection and let his, likewise, erupting dick fire-hose spray his spunky streamers far enough to hot-speckle our faces.

PART TWO

OTHERS

MIKE (AND ALAN)

My name is Mike. I'm a hustler.

Eleven inches of blond cock, all hard: that's the answer to the question asked me most often—Why did you get started hustling?—by the multitude passing in and out of my bedroom. The cock didn't, by the way, belong to me. It belonged to Alan Vandermere.

Alan and I were on the university frosh gymnastics team. From the beginning, we spotted for each other on the equipment and worked out together. We were both dubbed for varsity before the completion of our first semester. As good friends as we became, it was impossible for me not, eventually, to realize Alan was a hustler, as well as a full-time student.

I can't begin to count the number of times I've been asked to define the word hustler. I've always found it difficult, because there are so many variables. I mean, it's impossible to say that all of us have blond hair, green eyes, tanned skin, big cocks, and exceptional bodies; even though Alan did fit nicely into those particular categorizations. However, I know one other man who almost fits that description (his eyes are blue), who is married, has three kids, and would unhesitatingly make a concentrated attempt to beat the shit out of anyone who said he would even consider sex with another man, let alone be paid for it.

Nor is it possible always to use any number of phrases to qualify hustling which can be used to describe other professions. Like, *needs four years of college* which applies to the medical or legal professions. Granted, I have a university degree under my belt; but for every one of us who has one, I know ten others who don't.

Despite my inability to come up with an all-encompassing definition of just what is a hustler, there are a few generalizations possible which will hold true, at least in reference to the type of hustler I am, and the hustlers with whom I'm, personally, most familiar: we are male...we are dealing in a service for which we receive some form of compensation (not necessarily monetary)... we are good businessmen...we emphasize our good points ...we de-emphasize our bad points...we know our market ...we are not stupid...and we are generally sexually uninhibited.

By saying we are male, I'm referring to the word in its purely anatomical sense and not to what role we may or may not play in bed.

Whenever referring to a hustler, the automatic and correct assumption is that he's offering his body for sale. The possible differences between a mediocre hustler and a good one is, likely, the fact that, once the latter realizes he's a commodity on the open market, he has the business-sense to do everything possible to achieve higher sales and higher sales potential.

While cold cash is the usual means to exchange for offering services, this isn't necessarily always the case. I've known some of us who accept everything from travel to Lladra porcelains in payment for their company and services.

Successful hustlers are invariably good businessmen. We have to be. The product we're selling is us. I might state that all of us would be well to have a degree in marketing/advertising. The rudiments of knowing a product intimately, knowing how to package, promote, and successfully market it, would be of invaluable assistance to anyone in the profession. In fact, whether or not we, as hustlers, have marketing/advertising as our formal backgrounds, observation will usually always reveal that those of us who have been most successful have utilized basic business principles to get us where we are.

If we have good bodies, we wear the clothes to emphasize those: perhaps form-fitting t-shirts to show off the musculature of our chests, or designer jeans that hug and define our crotches or muscled legs. If we have good chests but flabby asses, then we wear the t-shirts but keep away from the tight-fitting trousers. If we have sunken chests and spindly legs, we find modes of dress that conceal those, and rely more on, say, our knacks for being amusing, being good conversationalists, or, yes, being fantastic in bed.

One of the hardest things, it seems, for us to do is decide just what is right for us as opposed to what we *think* is right for us. In hustling, more, perhaps, than in other professions, we have to be able to face realistically who and what we are. If we can't face the reality, then there's no way to go anywhere in this business. Once we know what we have to offer, we can select the existing market for it. To first select the market, and, then, try to revamp ourselves to fit it, is usually stacking the odds against us.

Assuming, when I use the word hustler, that I'm talking about a special breed of salesman who has moved deeper into the groove than picking up a few nickels and dimes, I can truthfully say that I have never met a successful hustler who was stupid. This certainly doesn't contradict my earlier observation that we don't all necessarily need a formal education. It does mean that if we don't have a formal education, we do have an inherent intelligence and the street smarts that allow us to see hustling not as an end, in and of itself, but as a means to an end.

Finally, and of great importance, we're basically sexually uninhibited males. The necessity for being such is obvious. Sex, after all, is the name of our game. No matter where we are in the hierarchy of selling our bodies, we must, by the pure nature of the game, be able to put out in bed. If we can't do that, or if we refuse to do that, then we've lost before even beginning.

Certainly, we are more uninhibited than ordinary people. That is because sex is our profession, and a certain extra proficiency in it is expected of us. This does not mean we, even those of us really successful, don't have our hang-ups. We do. However, those of us who are good at what we do will recognize those hang-ups and try to surmount them. An example to illustrate the point is what brings me back to Alan.

"A hustler has to be versatile," he told me prior to his turning all but one of his existing clientele over to me.

"I've realized that from the beginning, and I realize it now. Five years, I've been hustling. In all five of those years, I've never let anyone fuck me. I used to think no man had the price. I was wrong and really don't know just why I've been holding out my asshole as more sacred than any other part of my body."

A conjured picture of Alan offering up his butch virgin ass for some undisclosed financial reward was really too exciting to be believed.

"I've finally met someone," Alan continued. "He has money, and, what's more importantly, he's willing to spend a lot of it on me."

"You love him?" Even then, my question sounded extremely naïve.

"He's a pig," he answered frankly. "Love has nothing to do with it. Nothing at all. It's business. He's made me an offer...."

I waited for him to continue.

"I don't want that bastard to have first crack at my ass," Alan said. The tone of his voice, and the look in his eyes, delivered his intended message.

I've never been one who has to be hit over the head with a sledge hammer to see a proposition being made. I got up from my chair, walked the short distance to where he stood, and put one hand on each side of his waist. He put his hands on my face: four fingers along each cheek, and his thumbs outlined the corners of my lips. The way the light was coming through the window, I could see the green of his eyes and how wondrously the light caught in the blondness of his hair.

Without another word between us, we kissed. His lips were pliant yet firm; his tongue was probing but not gagging. His saliva tasted of the mint lozenge he had managed somehow to slip into his mouth.

I worked my hands behind his back, down over his ass, palming those resilient mounds as I simultaneously pulled his crotch tightly into mine. There was no mistaking the hardness of our erections.

His hands were no longer on my face but deftly undoing the buttons of my shirt. The next time we kissed, we were naked—chest against chest, belly against belly, and cock against cock.

We didn't go to the bedroom. At the time, I flattered myself that it was because he was as excited as I was. Since then, I've become a bit more cynical. Alan was too much of a pro to be consumed by any excessive passion. In hindsight, I can see him merely eager to perform a self-conceived ritual: a variation of the pagan sacrifice of the virgin's maidenhead. That's not to say that I've become so cynical as to suggest that Alan was utilizing me with the same total indifference as he might have utilized a ceremonial stone phallus for his purposes.

"My friend will want to fuck me dog-style," he said matter-of-factly. "I can read the bastard like a book."

With Alan on his hands and knees, I came at him from the rear. Even in my high state of excitement, I could marvel at the exquisiteness of his body, at the warm muscled quality of his flesh. Physical beauty and a will to succeed are both aspects vital to a person's success in this business.

"And he won't use lubricant," Alan said, anticipating my next question.

Still, I would have milked my penis for its natural lubricant if Alan's hand hadn't so quickly grabbed my cock and immediately positioned it between his buns. A quick backward rocking of his hips buried the head of my cock up his rectum.

I reared back on my knees, my fingers gripping tightly into the muscles of Alan's thighs. Pulling his butt back toward my pushing midsection, I felt my cock bend and then unbow deeply into the clutching warmth of his constricting anal slot. The hard muscles of my belly rammed the firm roundness of his butt's cheeks.

"Christ!" That was all he said.

Once I had my boner fully submerged, I paused, letting my right hand fall beneath his belly. Alan's cock was hard. I took his balls, pushing them between his legs until they met with mine. I squeezed our combined scrotums, feeling their excess flesh ooze through my fingers. A pleasantly gnawing ache spiraled upward from my groin to my lower belly.

I withdrew a couple of my cock inches from his body. My erection continued leaking during its sexual burial, and its second plunge was more easily achieved. His anal lining was a thousand vibrators at work on my naturally lubricated dick.

I released our balls, placing one hand on each of his ass cheeks. I pried his fleshy globes apart, pressing them outward along their mutually shared crease. The valley nestled between the mounds grew strands of blond hair. His asshole's mouth ovaled tightly about the circumference of my dick. I pushed my belly closer, watching another fraction of my cock concave his sphincter. I was entrenched, plowed as far into his clutching warmth as I would ever be. I leaned over his body, running my hands around his hips, enjoying the muscular ripples of his stomach and the hardness of his chest's pectorals. His nipples were hard beneath my fingers; rigid pinnacles that rose from the center of each quarter-size roseate.

My hand fisted his pole, dragging loose outer skin downward over solid inner core. His prick grew thicker; my grip had to widen in order to contain the cock's expanded girth.

I put my other hand to his dick, just above my other. I provided a long tunnel for his cock to fuck.

It seemed almost as if I were utilizing a toilet plunger for sexual purposes, his ass the suction cup positioned securely over my cock, his dick the wooden handle that I was using to keep the rubber affixed securely over my genitals.

There can be something extra exciting about fucking a virgin ass, whether it belongs to an eighteen-year-old boy, or to an eighty-year-old man. The knowledge that your cock is penetrating where no cock has been before it, your sperm flushing passages that haven't known the heated basting of other saline sexual douches, can be not only a physical turn-on but a psychological one. As far as my taking Alan's cherry, the experience for me was so intensely exciting that any lengthy prolongation of it by me quickly became impossible. Alan's asshole was just too sensuously tight, too alive with those spasms that were playing my quickly priming meat toward explosion.

Too quickly, in fact, to my way of thinking, I provided those few final lunges that triggered the flooding rush of my thick creamy cum from my sperm-ballooned balls.

During my moments of ecstasy, Alan's body collapsed beneath my frantic onslaught. His penis slipped one last time into the folds of my hands which were now squeezed beneath his belly by the weight of my exploding body on top of him. Even as my cream was jettisoning to fill his asshole, Alan's cum was squirting from his trembling erection. His deluge of sexual juice flooded the palms of my hands, soaked his belly, and smeared the rug beneath our climaxing bodies.

When I left his apartment that evening, it was the last I saw him. Two weeks later, I got a special-delivery packet from him. It had a foreign postmark. He had sent me the key to his apartment, plus a small notebook which contained his sexual clients, except for the one he was with. The notebook, also, contained carefully written comments after each name, as regarded that person's sexual preferences.

"My rent's paid up, there, for another two months," he wrote. "Take anything you want and leave the rest. Thought you might possibly make use of the enclosed notebook, too. If not, much luck anyway." Then, as an apparent afterthought, separated from the bulk of the main text, he had scribbled a quick: "His butt-fucking isn't really as bad as I expected."

DARREL (AND BRAD)

Okay, I'm Darrel, but let me take a few minutes to preface this with a little something about Brad. Granted, I know, this book isn't about him, or about hustlers like him, but I, at least, think he should be given a passing mention, if just because I'm one of the few successful hustlers who you're liable to meet who started out walking the streets, like Brad, and who would likely have ended up there if not for the luck of someone having picked me up, early in my hustling days, who knew someone, who knew someone, who ended up liking me enough to keep me around, on a pay-for-sex basis, long enough for me to realize, and capitalize on, the fact that the real money in this business didn't lie with me selling myself on some street corner.

Brad, after all, is the stereotypical hustler, not me. He's the figure most often written about in literature and most often seen in films: "the" midnight cowboy.

In fact, the average layman sees him as the very essence of the male body-selling profession. In truth, of course, walking the streets for money is the last method of entry into the trade that I would now ever recommend to anyone seriously contemplating hustling as anything more than a means of picking up a bit of spare change. A male walking the streets can be compared to the prostitute who sells her wares on the street corner. The really successful hustler is as far removed from the street corner as the expensive call girl is from the hooker on the sidewalk. But hey, what Brad does, he does very well. While most of his compatriots manage a few free meals, money for cigarettes, or a few drinks, Brad is managing a college education and a car—although the college isn't Ivy League and the car isn't an expensive Italian sports model. (Neither Ivy League school, nor expensive Italian sports car, by the way, is out of the reach of hustlers, like me, who have gone another route).

Faded Levi jacket. No shirt. Muscled, well-defined pectorals. Tanned and hairless chest. Faded jeans, sandpapered to gauze-thinness. Top button of trousers unfastened. No evidence of underwear—he isn't wearing any. Large basket viewed even from a distance. Black hair, cut short but not a military buzz-cut. Handsome rather than pretty: butch good looks. Boots, but not cowboy. Belt the same brown as his boots: an intricate interfacing of metal rings with leather.

He stands with his thumbs hooked into his belt, his fingers suggestively framing the area of his groin. He leans with his back against the wall, his left leg bent slightly due to the positioning of his heel against the building. He's not alone in his nightly vigil. Two other people share his side of the block. Two of them stand smoking and talking. Both of these others are younger, evidently high-school kids out for some fun and a little pocket money. They're definitely not professionals. Brad is.

Brad is an isolated little island among them, talking to no one. He knows one of the basic truths of hustling the streets for a dollar: most people who are cruising for a sex partner are paranoid about groups, and they shy away from them. Everyone hears the stories of homosexuals beaten up by straights who run in pairs.

I didn't meet Brad on his street corner, although I had seen him there several times before and have since seen him there. He was picked up by John—one of my regulars—who has an interest in "rough trade" and who has a decided knack in trolling for it.

John had paid my way and my expenses to a hotel in Vancouver, British Columbia. In my now long acquaintance with John, we've never once had sex. I always just come along as a third party to watch all of the action from the sidelines. I'm never able to tell whether I'm there because John gets an exhibitionist's thrill from performing before an audience of one, or whether my presence gives him some sort of release from concern that he might one day become the victim of one of those guys he so favors and so desires.

John never cruises with me along. He knows that any hustler is leery of entering a car with more than one passenger. If the buyer is often fearful of getting hit over the head by what he picks up, the hustler often has need to worry about the character he's getting in the car with.

John left me off at the hotel while he went out looking for what he wanted for the evening. It usually doesn't take him long, either. One evening, he spotted Brad on John's very first swing around the block.

John circled the block three times before he stopped. Some buyers are more direct, spotting what they want and zeroing in on it immediately. Such fast action often brands, from the onset, a beginner for the novice he is. A buyer experienced in cruising the streets will usually make at least one complete pass to check out the evening's total potential. Granted, he may spot someone right away who catches his fancy, but who's to say that there isn't someone five or ten times better on the other side of the block? One can argue that what one doesn't know can't hurt but that's damned ridiculous. If you're out shopping, you might as well get the most for your dollars. Why settle for milk when you might have the chance to sample some real cream?

I've had people complain to me that during their circling of the other three sides of a block, someone else zoomed on in and snatched some mighty fine specimen away. That could very well be the truth; however, they don't seem to recognize that as the guy in the car is checking out the merchandise, he's being sized up by the merchandise in turn. The potential buyers are noticed and categorized from their arrival, and an experienced hustler will wait for the prime buyer before going home with a second-rate substitute.

How does a street hustler size up a buyer? If the buyer has been around before, paid good money, been no trouble, a hustler can tell from past experience. If the buyer is new in the city, then, there's always his car to tell the hustler something about him.

A good number of people don't want to drive their expensive cars while cruising. Their reticence, of course, does have some merit, especially as expensive cars can attract not only interested hustlers but carjackers and the vice squad. No nervous businessman wants his license number jotted down as being seen continuously in a well-known homosexual pick-up area. However, no matter what anyone else will tell you, a street hustler will get into a Mercedes any day if his other chance is the potential offered by a Volkswagen and its driver. A street hustler, after all, like all of us in the business, is out to maximize his dollars in doing what he does. The odds are better that a hustler's price will be met, even exceeded, by Mr. Ugly in a Rolls, than by a Mr. Adonis in a Toyota. The car, therefore, is the first thing the kid on the street notices. If it's the right car, it'll likely get him in for a closer look at the clothes on the guy behind the wheel. If you're a buyer, don't count on your nice car, your good looks, and nice clothes, alone, though, landing you the street hustler you want. Money, after all, is the name of the game; most people in the trade would bed a dog if the price was right.

Don't think, either, that just because you're driving an expensive car, and/or wearing expensive clothes, that you're going to get gouged monetarily by the experienced street hustler. Actually, that's more likely to be the case if you're dealing with an amateur. Anyone seriously working the street looks for the possibilities for return business. He's, also, aware that some buyers compare notes. Any hustler worth his salt (or is it more apropos to say "worth his cream"?), will have a standard asking price and very rarely drift far from it. The amateur, of course, is another story. That is why everyone is usually better off when it's two professionals—both buyer and seller—playing the game.

As glamorous as street hustling often seems—and it does seem to exude a distinctive allure—don't expect any Cinderella endings, because it's not the venue that's going to provide any kind of Champagne existence. I know of very few of us who are top-paid professionals who can trace our roots back to the nickel-and-dime traffic of the streets. Most street hustlers get used and abused way too fast to survive long enough to make any real money.

"How old do you think I am?" Brad asked me. I had my glass and was sitting on the hotel couch. He sat down in the chair directly opposite. Automatically, his thighs opened; he'd practiced sitting that way for so long that the position managed to come across natural and not affected. He wasn't obviously self-conscious, either, about the impressive ridge his big dick made against his left thigh. The customer always prefers a preview of what he'll get—before any unveiling of it.

John had already told me that Brad was twenty-one. He looked twenty-eight if he looked a day; he isn't the type who ages well. I guessed he was about twenty-five, and I wasn't far off.

"I'm twenty-six," he said. "I've been hustling in one way or another for sixteen years."

I really don't think I looked dubious. After all, he wouldn't have been the first guy I knew who had come out, or been forced out, at a very early age.

"I started standing round the hustling areas for fun and finally got into some of those cars that were stopping. I lost my best years before I came to think of hustling as the business it is. I'm still kicking myself in the ass for realizing that fact so damned late. It puts me past my prime and still struggling like hell to get enough stashed away to complete college."

Brad got up from his chair and went to the liquor bottle.

"Have you known John long?" he asked suddenly.

About five years."

"You two ever make it together?"

"No."

"I didn't think so. You're not his type."

It didn't come out sounding derogatory, but he must have thought that it did, because he actually looked embarrassed.

"I mean, he likes his men to be used, abused, and look it. I'm lucky he came along. There's not much demand for guys like me."

I found myself immediately wondering what he looked like when he was ten and untouched, when he was thirteen and knowledgeable beyond his young years.

"You have to start young if you want to make it selling your body on the streets," he said. "And you have to know what you're doing from the get-go. You have only a few good years, and those are your young ones. Trying to start out making hustling pay as late as I did gets you nowhere. Oh, I'll make it through college. I'll do that, because I know if I don't, it's going to be one hell of a dead-end street waiting for me. I'll do it, because I was lucky enough to run into John, and a few others like him. If I ever make it big, it's going to have to be in some other profession—something in which I get a formal education."

Brad has had more success than the majority of those who join him nightly on the street corner; and Vancouver, remember, is a city relatively free of homosexual harassment by the police.

However, for those who still want to give this type of hustling a try, the procedure for beginning is quite simple. That's probably why so many attempt it at one time or another.

Find your nearest meat rack / hustling area. Every town usually has one, and it's often as easily located as asking for the directions in any local gay bar. Make sure the town you pick, however, is one of the larger ones. You have little chance of making your fortune in Dingelberry, Nebraska, even in one of the more lucrative forms of the hustling profession, let alone on a street corner. There has to be a good demand for your services; the larger that buying segment of the population, the better it'll be for you.

Spend some time watching the action on the street before you get actually involved in it. It's surprising how the rules of any game can usually be figured out by simple observation of how the other players proceed. Take a couple of evenings to scout out the turf and learn the prevailing ground rules.

For God's sake, have a price in mind when it's asked of you. Never get into a car until you're sure the buyer and you agree on what that price is. Make sure that you know what you'll be expected to do for the money, where you'll be going to perform the act, and how long you're going to be gone. Anyone of those can be used to determine or adjust your original asking price.

A serious suggestion, that has proven its merit in the past, is that anyone who is seriously thinking of entering into this aspect of the field for extra money should first have an unrelated job. Take on the hustling as a supplementary venture with hopes that it might blossom into something later. If you have the independence of not having to worry about money in the beginning, then you can set a higher price on your wares and wait for the word to get around that if anybody wants you that's exactly what they'll have to pay, or no go. If the word gets around that you've gone for ten dollars, because you were hungry, no one is going to pay more than ten dollars. They'll merely wait for the next time you're hungry.

Brad was paid more than he asked to be paid for that evening with John and me. John not only felt generous but has a tendency to put on I-have-money-to-spare (which he does) airs. John was driving his new Volvo when he picked Brad up. He was wearing his diamond ring, and his Brioni suit; he still was still wearing that expensive ring and that expensive suit when Brad yanked down John's pants, toppled John on the bed, and started to fuck him.

I watched, as usual, from a position not far away, judging as best I could whether or not the action was becoming a little rougher than even John desired. I had never yet encountered a time that my stepping in was necessary; although, just such a time did occur with John and another kid, in another town, in another room, about eight months later.

Brad's dick was a hard missile at work within John's quivering flesh. I was situated so that I could see the thick inches of Brad's cock as they withdrew and were then reinserted. Like John, Brad remained partially dressed; his dick had merely been pulled through the open fly of his trousers once John's pants had been yanked down.

Brad's belly pressed into John's quivering ass. I watched fascinated as John's ass cheeks were squashed beneath the continued bombardment of Brad's humping momentum.

John quivered even more beneath Brad, his voice begging for mercy in a tone that Brad and I both knew was anything but a desire for Brad to cease and desist before he had finished what he'd started.

I could easily imagine John's anal muscles contracting along the entire length of Brad's exquisitely shaped cock.

Brad withdrew his boner and placed it home again, in a series of staccato strokes that rocked the bed. His prick had apparently leaked a mess of natural lubricant; the bone-like shaft appeared smeared with translucence each and every time I caught a glimpse of it bridging the gap between Brad's lower belly and John's anus. The wet made Brad's pumping easier, smoother, and more powerful.

"It hurts!" John said, the word coming out in an almost undecipherable groan. "Good God, but it hurts."

Brad, though, was doing anything but hurting him and continued to poke away, faster and faster. The hustler's eyes took on a glassy sheen, his cheeks flushed. There was sweat on his forehead.

My cock was hard in my pants as I continued to witness the nonstop rise and fall of Brad over, and into, John's accepting body.

When Brad climaxed, he did so silently, continuing to pump his gallons of thick cream up John's ass even while John's penis was tracking the bedspread with its own pearly slime.

BRYAN (AND KYLE)

WHAT DO YOU DIG? Levis, leather, rubber, briefs, pose straps, jocks, nude, Gk. Fr. B&D, W/s, oil, S/M, toys, servitude, etc. My all mirrored well equip. game rm has this & more for fantasies furthered! Am skilled and versatile gdlkg bld, 25, end, bl eyes, well, 6'2", 175 lbs, 30" waist, 40" chest. Kurt....

ATTR BLD STUD. Bodybuilder, 25, 6' 178, college student will model nude or ??? Dig almost any scene. Will travel by hour or day....

LIKE EM BIG? Muscle builder Todd available as model or whatever turns you on. For best results, call from 9AM til noon, 1-10PM. All day Sat and Sun...

COLLEGE JOCK. Musc Phys. Hnky. Gdlking. Will relax your joints with experienced massage. Will also model. Into Levis

and leather if that's you're thing. Adaptable
to heaviest scene. Call Kyle....

You've all seen the advertisements. Perhaps, just as often, you've been tempted to answer them but never quite
got around to doing so. Perhaps, you've even wondered if
any of those ads do get answered. Are muscular studs with
heavy sex as near as your telephone, kept at a distance
only because you haven't quite gotten up the nerve to pick
up the receiver and summon them? Is there really that
dark, gdlking stud with bl eyes and tanned, well-built body
who is willing to give you that fantastic and wild rubdown
you've always wanted, or who will pose for you with
every conceivable kinky toy?

The answer is yes and no. Yes, in that's exactly how I
started out. No, in that the advertiser, more often than not,
has a higher regard for himself than the buyer ever will.
Many people who advertise probably should be prosecuted
for false advertising: the muscular construction worker
who wouldn't know a girder from a girdle—except that he
should be wearing the latter; that twenty-one-year-old boy
who hasn't seen twenty-one for over thirty years; that
blond, well-hung surfer who has never hung ten, in or out
of his pants. You could probably get a better massage from
a vibrator bed than from most of those "licensed" masseurs you find advertised in gay or underground newspa-
pers.

However, there are the exceptions to the rule. Occasionally, you're actually liable to come across a stud, like
me, who actually is a stud...an athlete who is an athlete...
a talented masseur who can expertly give you your mon-

ies' worth of massage. Oh, yes, the prizes are liable to be there if you're willing to go through the often tedious and expensive task of sorting through the flotsam and jetsam to find them.

The main problem for a buyer is, of course, that he's not able physically to see the merchandise before making some sort of commitment. The ugliest man alive can sound like an Adonis in an ad, even over the telephone. Unlike the street corner, you don't see what you're getting until he's standing in your doorway, expecting to be asked inside (your room and, sometimes into you). At least, on the streets, a buyer can check out the merchandise before getting it as far as where he's staying. And let's face it, in America's youth-oriented society, no one is going to advertise himself as an ugly, cross-eyed, fifty-year-old faggot dwarf, even if he is one. Don't be so naive as to expect him to do so.

For the person who is interested in selling, rather than buying, newspaper advertising has advantages over peddling your body on the streets. Its main advantage is obvious. It's far more convenient to sit home by the telephone, waiting for a trick to call, that it is to be walking the streets at midnight looking for one. Yet, since you're not out on view, it is, also, impossible for any buyer to compare your actual physical qualifications with the existing competition. A buyer must rely, instead, upon your writing ability and the way you put yourself across in a advertisement and on the phone—neither of which often has anything whatsoever to do with how you might actually stack up to any other hustler. Since it's not necessary for those who hustle in this manner to even make an appearance, prior to their arrival before the buyer, there will be far more ads placed than people found nightly on any prime hustling corner. Even if a guy who advertises has all the proper physical qualifications for satisfying, he suddenly finds himself unfairly thrust into competition with a score or more people who don't have those qualifications but aren't averse to pretending that they do. The latter count heavily on that aspect of human nature which seems to make it pretty difficult for some people to say no to someone they've personally summoned, even if that person isn't what was really ordered.

Next to walking the streets for a living, the independent who gets involved in the modeling-masseur route to hustling has entered one of the easiest doorways to body selling. For the monetary output necessitated to place an ad, in comparison to the possible financial rewards to be realized, on an hourly basis, the rewards can be well worth the time and effort.

However, it has been my personal experience that those who make it big in hustling do so by gathering together a regular clientele. Getting a group of regulars, when going the advertising route, isn't the easiest row to hoe. Most of those who answer those ads are the types who think variety is the spice of life. A hustler might be good for one or two sessions with them, but the buyers who peruse the advertising sections for models and masseurs tend to be a fickle lot and always anxious to move on and sample that next new bld, bl-eyed construction stud with his proclaimed 44" chest, 31" waist, and 14" biceps and/or penis.

Let's keep in mind that the majority of hustlers who advertise are independent operators. They do not have either syndicate or corporate backing. The modeling agency or massage parlor—which often advertises—is something else again. I wasn't long in the business before I was taken on by a "modeling" agency, and I doubt very much whether I'd be where I am today, head of my own agency, if I'd remained an independent who relied entirely on my personally placed advertisements for my success.

Kyle is an independent. Meaning that he places his own advertisements at his own expense, makes his own arrangements on the phone to meet clients, reaps the entire financial rewards without paying a commission or percentage to a third person or sponsoring organization.

I read Kyle's ad and called him. While I don't usually personally recruit my models, any more, relying on others to do it for me, I haven't stopped it completely; maybe because I know that I haven't gotten where I am today by not always keeping personal involvement and a close ear to my industry.

Anyway, unlike many other people who have been summoned as a result of reading an ad, Kyle was one of the few, like I was, who turned out exactly as advertised. He even plays football at Southern California.

"Sure, I could lie," Kyle said, "but what in the hell would that prove? In the long run, I figure it would be detrimental. What happens if I come all this way, and you open the door to find I'm a forty-year-old fat man? You'd tell me to get lost, and I'd be out my fee, plus car fare."

I was staying at the house of a long-time friend (one-time client) in Beverly Hills. Kyle came by the house. It was evening. My friend and his lover (why my friend is now just a friend and not a client), had flown to San Francisco for the weekend. They had left me in complete charge of the house and its three bedrooms.

Kyle and I had taken care of most business details over the telephone. Asked whether I wanted him as a masseur or as a model, I'd answered that I probably wanted him for both. Asking someone to strip for modeling, before moving on to the massage, is a great way to get the hustler quickly naked without going through any awkward rigmarole. As a matter of fact, that's usually why you'll find modeling mentioned in one and the same ad as massage. Where it's logical that a model disrobe for posing, a legitimate session of massage won't necessarily require the masseur to join his subject in taking off his trousers. That is if you actually end up wanting to see him stripped. There have been times when an advertisement has been such a gross exaggeration of the merchandize that all I did, as soon as I opened the door, to see the guy in question, was to shut the door in his face. Kyle is one of those exceptions who make all of the disappointments seem suddenly worthwhile. Immediately, I saw indications of his well-toned physique underneath his clothes, and I was sure it would be well worth the unveiling.

I was right. His chest is a playground of muscular definition; his entire body is an exquisitely chiseled work of seeming perfection. He has a hard, washboard belly that sprouts a profusion of hair from its belly button to his upper thighs. His cock and balls are bull-like. The blond hair on his head tumbles in an unruly mass almost into his eyes. His eyes are gray. His cheeks are dimpled.

We started out with the photographic session. Kyle stepped easily into the role that I asked him to play. I had dug my camera out of my luggage, and Kyle's posing looked professional. I later found out that he gets a little extra cash by posing for art classes at the university. Aside from being professional in posing, he was—as I was to learn, to my pleasant surprise, as we moved on—also proficient in the art of massage. He is good to such a degree, as a matter of fact, that I quickly found myself forgetting that I had read his advertisement in a gay newspaper and could realistically expect more from him than just a good back rub.

"You answer the ads very often?" Kyle asked.

By that time, we were both stripped. I was lying on the bed. Kyle's hands are large, strong, and powerful. So, I might add, are his cock and his balls.

"You think I'm a novice at this?" I asked.

"Not necessarily a novice," he said. "But why else pay me for something you can obviously have countless people give you for free—or pay you for—unless it's just something different to do for temporary kicks? Only an idiot would ever imagine that my life is filled with well-hung studs and beautiful people like you."

Whether walking the streets, running an ad, having "made it" with that sought-after penthouse with the Italian sports car waiting in the garage, a hustler learns to expect days and nights of sex with less than perfect partners. The young, the well-hung, the beautiful, don't have to put out the cash to get their asses plugged, or their cocks sucked. Two to one, they don't even have the money to pay out even if they wouldn't be averse to doing so."

His fingers kneaded the flesh of my back, moved downward toward my butt. I felt my cock rock-hard beneath my belly and against the sheet.

On my back, with my eyes open, I saw the state of his erection at one and the time he saw the state of mine. We were both smiling.

"We've wasted a good deal of time, you know that, don't you?" he said.

He wrapped his hand around my stiff penis, and milked it of pre-cum that soaked his thumb and forefinger where they parenthesized the flare of my prick's corona.

"Let's see if we can't take care of this particular stiff joint," he said with a wide grin and what was probably his stock line.

He straddled my supine body on the bed. He sat so that the crease of his ass couched the hardness of my penis. He leaned his upper body forward, kissing my neck. He ran the warmth of his lips and tongue down my chest. He found one of my nipples, chewing gently on its growing hardness before surrendering it in favor of the other.

His tongue left my chest, finally, and licked a swath of spit to my six-pack abdominals where it probed my navel and wet down the hair that haloed the indent.

His mouth slid even farther down my body. His buns slipped to release their sandwiching of my cock, leaving my boner exposed on my tummy. His healthy balls pooled upon mine; his erect spire jutted so far upwards between his thighs that the massive head of his dick actually pillowed itself upon the cupping of his navel.

As his tongue licked its path nearer and nearer my drooling penis, his knees worked open my thighs. I willingly opened my legs farther to let his body rest comfortably in between.

My penis was long and hard, and its whole bulky shaft was throbbing. He touched its tip with his pointed tongue. My massive tower of meat jerked. His face fell over my circumcised cock head, entrapped it within his mouth. His tongue massaged it with the same expert precision with which his fingers had previously worked the taut muscles of my neck, shoulders, and back.

He bowed his head to take in additional inches of my hard meat. His spit drooled all over my cock as my dick slowly but surely disappeared completely within his face. The head of my dick was buried deeply in his throat, having been sensuously deflected off his bony palate and into that hugging passageway. My cock pulsed and throbbed wildly as his lips forcefully gummed its very roots.

He was good, very good. When one gives head for a living, like I've done and still, occasionally, do, that person is usually surprisingly willing to give credit where credit is due. Kyle hadn't given the slightest indication that he might ever choke on his sizable mouthful. I lifted my hips so my pubic hair wrapped even more completely around his lips and nose.

His hands slipped beneath my ass, his fingers cupping those twin globes. His hold lifted my pelvis even closer into his sucking. His mouth commenced to move up and down with swift, sure motions. His tongue was a whip working over the entire mass of my thickened cock meat. His lips fed my manhood in and out of his mouth and throat. He suctioned my bulbous cock head farther within him, his vacuuming a force of nature that pulled on the tip of my dick as his tongue simultaneously bathed it.

My leg muscles tightened. If Kyle automatically sensed my impending eruption, he must have realized there would be more where this one came from, because he didn't try to hold it off. In fact, he increased and magnified the intensity of his sucking to make my dork throb all the more, grow thicker and heavier.

I put my hands on his shoulders, digging my fingers into the solid muscle I found there as my hips bounced within his still-gripping hands. My cock thrust deeply within the sensuous warmth of his oral sheath.

I blew my guts, releasing a good pint of boiling sperm. Wad after delicious wad of it jettisoned down Kyle's throat. My body trembled as I watched through passion-blurred eyes as Kyle frantically attempted to keep himself securely anchored over my exploding penis. His fingers dug deeply into my butt, and his head rode out my last convulsive shudders.

Eventually, I asked him the one question I put to all my fellow hustlers, under similar circumstances, or otherwise. Do they make a good living doing what they do?

"Hell no," Kyle said with a you-have-to-be-kidding laugh. His body was hot and slightly sweaty beside mine. "Does anyone really make a good living out of just hustling? Oh, I know I've heard about them, read about them, but I've never met them. I doubt that I ever will. I hustle because it helps me supplement the money I earn during the summer when I'm not in school. After school, though, I'll need to find a real job to get me the retirement benefits hustling would never provide me."

I gave him my card, as head of my modeling agency, and told him to call me. I know potential when I see it. Whether or not Kyle has the smarts to take advantage, and make the most out of the opportunity I've provided, I'll have to wait and tell you later.

LAWRENCE

I attend one of the West Coast's better known universities. I have an apartment not far from campus, in a moderately priced, but nice, rental district. I supplement my monthly allowance from my parents by catering to the sexual requests of six regular johns: two of whom live in the same city, four of whom travel through on a frequent basis.

One Wednesday morning, I got a call from Henry. Henry is a young salesman for a leading can company who I was introduced to through mutual friends. Henry was scheduled to be in town for a stopover early that afternoon and wondered if he might get together with me for a quickie between plane flights. Although I was scheduled for a math class between two and three, I consented to the appointment, calling a friend to ask her to sit in on the lecture and take notes.

At two o'clock, Henry was at my apartment, and I was waiting for him, wearing only a robe. We'd been through the routine so many times before that there was little need for delay. Henry likes to get fucked by big cock, and I come sufficiently well-endowed to satisfy even Henry's penchant for penile bulk. We retired immediately to the bedroom.

Since Henry always enjoys timing his masturbations to coincide with my eruptions up his ass, he quickly stripped. He then got down on all fours. I produced a tube of lube with which I greased my penis. Putting the tube aside, I knelt down behind Henry and put the head of my dick to the target. Five seconds later, most of my ten inches were lost up Henry's tightly clenching asshole while the man's right hand was busy stoking his erected meat.

Henry left at four, and I went to a late afternoon lab that got me home at shortly before six. I was met at the door by Ryn. Ryn isn't one of my regulars. He's a fellow student and a friend—actually a good friend. Disobeying hustling's prime directive—don't give away anything you can sell—I'm having a half-assed affair with Ryn on the side. However, knowing that I had another firm appointment lined up for that evening with a regular, I was, at first, reluctant to accept Ryn's overtures for sex. However, suspecting that he would be content with being top man in a quick fuck, I decided to oblige. I got belly-down on the bed, felt his cock pounding up my butt, and managed, through sheer willpower, to keep from any ejaculation of my own.

Ryn left, and I showered and shaved in preparation for the arrival of Martin.

Martin is my regular for Wednesday evenings. I was still in my robe when he arrived. It was because of him that I had been so careful in conserving my cum with Ryn. Martin is very demanding, paying good money to suck my cock to three consecutive orgasms to coincide with only one for his. As I had already blasted once that afternoon up Henry's butt, I hadn't wanted to be hard-pressed to supply Martin with his Wednesday evening's expected sperm-quota.

At nine o'clock, his mouth was firmly anchored over my cock, and I was frantically pumping my hips while simultaneously thanking God that the forces which were again rising in my balls, for my third climax with Martin, would soon see the session over and done. His dick in his hand, he expertly timed his one climax of the evening to coincide with my third, finally arrived, expulsion of salty seed that he sucked right on down.

By ten o'clock, Martin was gone. The extra cash he left upon leaving gave every indication that he was more than satisfied with my performance.

At ten-five, I was in bed. I was quite content to bag all studying and set the alarm clock for six the next morning so that I could go over my notes before attending an 8:15 chemistry class. I had just turned out the light when the phone ran.

Ten minutes later, I was letting Craig into my apartment. Craig, realizing that his usual session was regularly scheduled for Saturday, wasn't put off by my candid confession that I would be lucky to get another hard-on at any time during the rest of the night. Although Craig usually prefers my dick hard and up his ass, he was willing to pay a good price for me to suck him off. Craig's mother-in-law hadn't been feeling well that evening, and Craig's wife had decided to go spend the night with her ailing mother. Craig was reluctant to let that opportunity for a little illicit man-on-man sex, with me, go untapped.

When Craig left, I, within less than twelve-hours, had fucked and sucked, and, in turn, been fucked and sucked. Although this type of an evening is hardly a nightly occurrence for me, they're known to occur in any successful hustler's life.

For some reason, the fear of AIDS and/or other venereal diseases, by us hustlers, and by our clients, seems to come and go in cycles. There are periods wherein everyone is careful to wear rubbers, even when on the receiving end of a blowjob; there are other times when no customer seems in the least concerned about the dangers of barebacking and wants to do it, whether as top or bottom. While it's important that I always pay particular attention to my health, if I want to keep on being successful in this business until my retirement, it's even more important to do so whenever a no-rubber cycle is in effect, especially if I succumb to the temptation of making an extra buck or two, assuming, rightly or wrongly, that all johns requesting bare-backing have a clean bill of health.

Just because a regular customer is "clean" of disease, during one visit, doesn't necessarily mean that he'll be clean the next, or the next. Like an "ideal" lover who still sometimes cheats on his other half, any one of my regulars can philander outside our hustler-client business relationship. For the john, such an opportunity just might arise out of the blue, and he succumbs to it; or, he might have it preplanned to try and determine whether one of my competition meets his needs better than I do. Someone, like I, whose part-time lover, on the side, isn't likely monogamous, either, has even higher odds of coming down with something venereal.

For homosexuals, in general, supposedly noted for their promiscuity, it has always been recommended we get a checkup at least once every six months. While I know, for a fact, that not all of us are the nymphomaniacs we're so often painted to be, a six-month checkup is undeniably a very good idea. Since I'm a successful hustler, as well as a homosexual, I'm likely to go see a doctor even more often. I only need get stuck once (figuratively, or literally) to end up being sorry for the rest of my life, all of my money-earning days over and done. Along with the danger of AIDS, there are all of those new and hybrid forms of venereal diseases being brought back into this country by GIs from the Middle East. Therefore, it behooves me to get my plumbing periodically examined by a professional, and to protect it, at every opportunity, if I really want to make sure I'm as safe as I can be in the business I'm in.

Finding a doctor isn't quite as hard for a hustler as it might at first seem. The phone book is full of doctors. Finding one with whom a hustler feels comfortable is probably a little more difficult. For people who are gay, they often feel that a doctor who is, likewise, gay has a certain empathy with them and is, thus, better suited to cater to their needs. That said—there are gay doctors who don't look any more favorably on homosexual prostitution than straight doctors do. In the end, the selection of a doctor, by a hustler, or by any gay, is, like the selection of a deodorant or cologne, a purely personal thing.

For instance, personally, I find I'm much more comfortable discussing my medical problems with my straight doctor than I would ever be in discussing them with a gay doctor. Of course, this might well be because I don't want any heart-to-heart talks with my doctor. I don't want to cry on his shoulder. Certainly, I don't want to compare tricks or notes on the gay community. What I want is a reputable medical man who is capable of giving me correct medical information, correct diagnosis, correct treatment, and service. That's exactly what my doctor provides. I would hardly call him my bosom buddy, and I'm not even really sure that he approves of my homosexuality, let alone my hustling. The point is, though, he never makes my homosexuality, or my hustling, an issue; although, it has become standard procedure that I provide him with rectal and oral swabs each time I come in for a checkup. The few times I have been unfortunate enough to come down with gonorrhea, my doctor has dealt with the Public Health people for me, and he has done it in a professional and business-like manner. I found him on the university staff, my freshman year, when I suffered from a bad case of the flu, and I have remained with him since he went into private practice during my senior year.

It's often the easiest to stick with the doctor you've had since an early age. It has been my experience that few long-visited family doctors are likely as stupid as not to have at least suspected any long-time patient's homosexual tendencies, maybe even before the patient did. As all conversations with a doctor should be held by him in the strictest of confidence, there's no real reason why any hustler shouldn't just up and ask any long-time family physician to schedule periodic VD and AIDS examinations. Of course, many hustlers would just as soon not have the same doctor, who treats them for VD, also, treat their siblings and parents. This is, of course, quite understandable.

I really suspect that locating a regular physician can hardly be as difficult as some people would have me believe. Although I've had mine for the past ten years, during the course of those years, I've continually heard of several doctors who treat other hustlers; others who are gay and have gay patients; others who are straight but could care less about a person's sexual preferences. If, for any reason, I should suddenly find my doctor unsuitable, I doubt it would take me long to come up with a reliable substitute.

If, however, a hustler is really at a loss, I suggest he merely ask any of his gay friends, or his fellow hustlers, where they go for medical treatment, or stop by his local gay service organization. Usually in any fair-size city, there are gay groups which regularly schedule VD and AIDS checks and that can certainly steer any hustler in the right direction.

Whatever, whenever, any hustler does regularly need to see a doctor—and do get complete examinations regularly. How regularly, of course, is something everyone must judge for himself, depending upon the frequency of sexual contacts, and how unprotected the sex is. I know some hustlers who would be safe by going once a month. I know others who should probably go as often as once a week.

If, for any reason, a hustler should suspect he's caught something before he's found a personal physician, then he should go to the Public Health facility nearest him, and let them give him a checkup. I'm always disconcerted by how many people in the gay community seem to think that Public Health is some ogre out to get them. Granted, they're hardly the friendliest people around, and the nurses often wield syringes with a veritable vengeance, but they can check someone for a disease, and, if they find it, they can often provide the cure.

For God's sake, a hustler shouldn't sit around thinking that just because he doesn't have any symptoms that he's disease-free. Some of this new stuff that is coming in from overseas doesn't give any warning, by way of symptoms, until they're full-blown.

I had the shit scared out of me not all that long ago, in that I thought for sure I'd come down with one of those weird strains of VD. I'd fucked around with this colonel just in from Afghanistan. Because he came highly recommended and had, likewise, been in the Medical Corps, I figured he'd be clean, for sure.

God, he had one hell of a big dick. It was really a beauty. Does beautiful sound like a stupid adjective for a penis? I guess so, but I can't think of any other way to describe it. It was big: a good ten inches long. Damn, it was thick. It had this head that had the cleanest no-scar circumcision I've ever seen; and I've seen a lot of cut cock in my time to know what's out there.

He really liked sex. Christ, but that guy was horny! The way he fucked my mouth and ass, I could have easily believed that he hadn't had sex for all the time he was overseas. I mean, he really went to town. I'll bet I was shitting and burping his spunk for a good week after he had at me.

He really liked getting blown. And I'm pretty good at giving head. I just opened my mouth for that damned thing of his and swallowed it right on down to its thick roots. He went absolutely out of his fucking tree. It was really exciting to see this big butch soldier whimpering like a baby every time he shot another load.

I knew I'd never forget him. Then, I got a damned blister on my dick, and I knew for damned sure I'd never forget him. You do know the type of things those bastard GIs bring back with them, these days? So much for someone highly recommended, and in the Medical Corps, being implicitly trusted! I was cursing that fucker and his big dick all of the way to my doctor's office.

So much for my success as a hustler, was what I was suddenly thinking. Though I do have a sizable nest egg, it wouldn't last me long if I had to start buying and taking enormous drug cocktails

The doc took a bunch of tests and said there was nothing for me to worry about. He gave me some salve, and the sore was gone in a week. God bless the doc! Every hustler should, in fact must, have one.

JERRY (AND TRUCKER)

Take it from this successful hustler—

There are homosexual businessmen, actors, butchers, bakers, possibly even candlestick makers. There are homosexual painters, welders, doctors, lawyers, possibly even Indian chiefs. There are, also, yes, homosexual policemen. However, as someone who successfully sells my body for a living, I wouldn't count on ever meeting up with a homosexual policeman in any capacity where he can be of any help to me. Of all the gay policemen I've know, and there have been a few, all but one of them have kept their sexual identities pretty much under lock and key and couldn't, by any fair stretch of the imagination (yours, mine, theirs), be expected to stand up on a soap box and lecture on the bad treatment given homosexuals—let alone given hustlers like me—by "men dressed in blue."

If any policeman, gay or straight, comes knocking on my door to take me away and book me, chances are very good that I'm not going to persuade that cop to do otherwise by me pulling down my pants and grabbing my ankles, or by my pulling down his pants and grabbing his dick. If I ever even suggested to a cop that he might be willing to compromise, in order to keep me from going to jail, I'd likely end up in far hotter water than I was already in.

If I've finished sucking off a new client, and his cum is still hot and salty on my tongue when he pulls out his ID and badge and informs me that he's a member of the vice squad, I don't assume that just because he's shared with me one of man's most intimate moments that he's going to be any more understanding, than any other policemen, when confronted with a "queer." In fact, if he's gone so far as actually to let me carry the sexual act to completion, the chances are excellent that he'll be even quicker in his condemnation of me, and in full denial of that completed sex act. With it being my word against his, I stand about as much chance in court as a hard cock stands of staying hard in the face of both its balls being threatened with castration.

When it comes right down to any advice I might give another hustler, or a potential hustler, in regard to the police, it would be to avoid them, or any contact with them, as you would avoid the plague. Most policemen are law-abiding citizens, and prostitution in the United States is still against the law. Hustlers, like I, have long realized that policemen take a dim view of homosexuality, in general, and of homosexual prostitution, in particular.

These days, before I even touch an individual, I usually make sure that he comes highly recommended by one or, hopefully, even more of my other clients. Utilizing this referral method is far safer for me than having sex with just any Tom, Dick, or Harry, who might knock at my door with a bulging cock and a bulging wallet in his pants. Of course, such selection is a luxury that few of us in the trade can actually enjoy 24/7. If you're a hustler who has to make do with a nightly stance on some street corner, you can't afford to ask everyone who approaches if he comes complete with character references. However, since you can't, more hustlers from the streets end up in jail than those of us who conduct our business elsewhere.

A hustler shouldn't assume, though, that just because he's set himself up in an apartment, or is employed by an agency, that his chances are one-hundred percent of being passed over when it comes to police harassment. Recent crackdowns on male prostitution rings operating under the guise of talent agencies bear witness to every hustler's vulnerability, even mine.

Like everything illegal, the monetary gains from hustling can be sizable and, more importantly, tax free. Naturally, such a thing will attract certain underworld factions, and, these, in turn, attract the police. It can safely be assumed that the police are not interested in busting the independent hustler as much as they are in cracking down on major prostitution, gay and straight, as moneymakers for organized crime. But if the individual body seller is ferreted out, along the way, you can bet your ass that his ass will be busted.

Sometimes, luckily for us, there are to be found, in occasional police departments, certain less than honest policemen who'll often find it in their best interest to let money cross their palms rather than have to bother hauling our asses into jail on a regular basis. I, for one, am in total agreement with anyone in our business who decides to pay crooked cops whatever they ask "for protection." It's usually an affordable pay-off, in that the cops don't want to kill the goose that can regularly keep laying such a golden egg. What's more, the money is well spent if it keeps us from having to worry about constant police interference in our business and in our lives Besides, if we don't pay, we'll find ourselves pulled out of our beds, or yanked off the street, at all hours of the night and day. Such frequent interruptions will make our customers paranoid. And paranoid customers aren't customers for long.

Those of us into any level of hustling should expect to be hauled off and booked at a police station at least once in our careers. There are always the exceptions to the rule, but it's ridiculous to assume, from the beginning, that you, if a hustler, are going to be lucky enough to be one. The best way to survive the ordeal is to plan for it. And make no mistake about it, it is an ordeal. You are photographed, you are fingerprinted, you are sometimes asked to strip completely to see if you have any concealed weapons, or drugs, secreted anywhere, including up your asshole. All of this is usually done as a means of degradation, rather than for any real search for guns, tire irons, or contraband. It supposedly confirms to you, in no uncertain terms, that you are completely subservient to the law of the land and to those—the police—who enforce it. You can expect a lot of wisecracking to go along with this process. There will inevitably be crude remarks made about your anatomy: the tightness of your ass, the size (or lack of size) of your dick, *et cetera…ad nauseam.*

Certainly, a hustler should always have a lawyer and, when arrested, use the one allowed telephone call to call that lawyer. And, the hustler should refuse to say anything, or sign anything, until his lawyer arrives. Let his lawyer do the talking. That's what lawyers are paid for.

I highly recommend that a hustler always have enough cash or credit cards on his person to post, immediately, whatever bail is established. Granted, size of bail differs per localities, but he can check with any lawyer, bail bondsman, or directly with the police, to find out the standard in his area of operation. There's nothing more frustrating than keeping cash reserves with a friend, or with a lawyer, only to discover that, when the money is needed, the friend, or the lawyer, isn't immediately available. It's particularly disconcerting to know the money is "there", but it can't be gotten to, and, thus, results the hassle, supposedly planned to be avoided, of being thrown into the drunk tank for a very long time (even the shortest of times, there, seemingly long times).

When I was first starting out in the business, I was picked up by a plain-clothes policeman while I was hustling a hotel bar. To make a long story short, I said yes when this guy offered me a drink, and I said yes when he asked me to have sex.

I was thrown into the drunk tank. I called my lawyer, but he wasn't in. I left a message on his answering service.

It's true what they say about the high possibility of getting raped when you're in jail. There's always someone there, usually another detainee, who thinks he has the right to jab his cock up your man pussy. One old drunk tried to get me to suck on his cock, and one old Negro wanted to fuck me. It wasn't too pleasant. Of course, the police didn't helped matters. The cop who put me in the cell made a special announcement that I'd been picked up for trying to blow one of the vice squad. That was enough to set all the horny bastards to wondering if they could get a free piece of my tail.

I tried to ignore the wisecracks, sticking off in my own little corner of the cell. Also, I kept telling myself that all of the horror stories I'd heard were just a bunch of bull-shit. It wasn't as if I was off in some maximum security prison. Christ, it was just the local drunk tank.

About the time, however, that I had resigned myself to the fact that I was going eventually to have to fight, or of-fer a couple of them the ass they wanted, the cops did me a big favor and obliged by dropping Trucker in with me.

"Here's another cocksucker to keep you company, cocksucker," the cop said. And you can bet your sweet ass that I was glad to see that other cocksucker arrive, in that Trucker is one of those guys who can handle himself in any crowd. It didn't take him more than a couple of min-utes to size up the situation and offer me support. We'd met before. He had once had a trick who had wanted a three-way, and Trucker had asked me to be the third; there had been a couple of other times when we'd bumped into each other at parties.

With Trucker in jail with me, it was easier to make it through the night.

Next day, my lawyer had both Trucker and me out on bail and apologized for not being able to make it happen sooner. I was magnanimous in accepting his apologies, since my ass hadn't been ripped in a gang bang. Trucker was grateful, too, because he hadn't really expected the favor of my standing his bail. Trucker isn't the type who bothers with having a lawyer. He figures that he can take care of himself, and he usually can.

We went back to my apartment for coffee and ended up having sex. Though nothing had happened with all those drunks, there had been something exceptionally exciting about having spent a whole night listening to a bunch of them asking us how we'd like to take their big cocks rammed up our rosy-reds. Since then, I've always been able to appreciate the way some of my clients get so turned on by me talking dirty to them.

It's really a shame that two hustlers, like Trucker and I, don't get together for sex with each other more often. It's usually a very good experience whenever it happens. Each has so long been programmed to please the client that when two professionals get it on together, it's usually really wild. There's not so much of this ego trip, of, "Let's see what you can do to please me," as it is, "Let's see what I can do to make a pro like you respond as if you haven't been through it all sixty-million times before." I think, because Trucker had stood between me and any jail-rape attempts, I was even more bent on pleasing him.

I don't know if Trucker had any forethought about the sex game as we ended up playing it, or not; I sure as hell didn't. All I know is that when I knelt down in front of his hard and naked cock, and he said he was a cop, and I was a fucking queer good only for sucking his prick and balls, I was ready to play. Of course, after all we'd been through, the previous night, and even before that, I knew there was no way Trucker could ever be even a clandestine member of vice. It was all just part of a charade; after all we'd been through, we just automatically felt it would make our session even more enjoyable, than it would otherwise be, by doing a bit of role-playing. I wouldn't want to get involved in any psychological analysis of the scene, as we acted it out, beyond admitting that our experiences of the night before had made us pretty ticked off at the police. It was erotic for Trucker to take on the role of a cop who really enjoyed a homosexual romp while pretending that he didn't. It was equally erotic for me to pretend that I was the cocksucking hustler who could and would make even a law-abiding civil servant go weak in his knees.

"Suck me, queer bastard!" he said.

I didn't go for his cock, at first, but pushed my face against his balls, feeling their wiry hair against my nose, lips, and cheeks. He has a good set of weighty nuts; they are a good handful; they are, also, a good mouthful as I was to discover when I pursed my lips against his scrotum and sucked in both of his gonads.

"You like sucking cop balls, faggot?" he asked me, putting his ham-like hands in my hair and letting them ride my head over his testicles. I washed both of his nads with my saliva, mashed them gently into each other, and rolled them against the insides of my cheeks.

I put my hands around Trucker's well-formed ass cheeks, working my fingers into the crease until I found the pucker of his asshole waiting in the steamy dampness.

"You think this cop's going to let himself get finger-fucked by the likes of you?" he asked; however, he didn't try to stop the insertion of my finger. As a matter of fact, he actually reared his hips backward so that it was more his action, than mine, which sunk half my finger up his rectum.

With my finger probing even deeper up Trucker's bung, I surrendered his balls and licked my way up his vein-latticed cock shaft. Immediately, I ovaled my lips over his fist-shaped cock corona and felt his hands pushing me down over the prize.

"Come on, faggot, see if you can take a mouthful of pig dick!"

Trucker shoved his hips forward, jabbing more of his cock into my face. His prick head rammed against my palate and deflected down into my throat. At the same time that his boner was disappearing down my gullet, my fingers were playing with his spit-drenched balls. Already his scrotum had achieved the consistency of a dried prune, gathering both of its nuts up towards the base of his swollen prick.

My tongue wrapped his cock shaft, the muscles of my throat contracting about his huge piece of hard meat. My nose pressed into his lower belly. The taste of his dick was delicious. The feel of his dick, fucking my face, was exciting beyond belief.

My mouth was moist and warm and swimming with spit. I bucked my head faster over his priming erection. My throat muscles tensed, strained with their milking of his enormous phallic pap. His cock throbbed within my throat. His fingers clamped hard into my scalp.

"Cop cum, cop cum, cop cum," Trucker chanted and grunted, feeding me a deluge that flooded my throat. I twisted my finger up his rectum, feeling his walnut-size prostate through the lining of his asshole.

Later, after I'd fucked him, and the sex and the game playing was almost finished, he told me I should really take karate if I was going to stay in the flesh-peddling business.

"I might not be there next time you're picked up," Trucker said, "and getting raped is never any damned fun."

Trucker's suggestion is one of the best tips any hustler can give another. Take up one of the martial arts! It won't keep you from getting pulled in by the police, but it will keep you safer in any jail cell. Also, it will protect you from any number of the other kooks you're apt to run into in this business. I wouldn't have ended up as successful as I am if I hadn't followed Trucker's suggestion.

MALCOMB (AND SAM)

Susan Kale was a prostitute in London, England. In her autobiography, *The Fire Escape*, she says something that can be tweaked to apply equally to a good many of us men in the trade: So far from having a good time, a street-walker lives in perpetual fear. Fear of men, of not finding a man, of the police, of being abandoned in outlandish places, of being robed or murdered, and of the night when he will discover he's too old.

Hustling and its female equivalent are not all they're cracked up to be. I often wonder just what it is about prostitution, especially male prostitution, which holds such a fascination for so many gay people. I often suspect that the mysticism evolves directly from the fact that someone who can get money for his body must have something worth selling. A good many narcissistic people, therefore, feel that a receipt of cash for their services merely reaffirms their high opinions of themselves.

In actuality, hustling is usually far from glamorous, although it certainly may have its glamorous moments. There is the money. There's the good fun in getting to know some neat people. There's the possibility of doing a lot of traveling, and there is the chance of retiring at an early age. However, often the money doesn't fully compensate for the degree of degradation you think you've been forced to endure; most of the people aren't really fun to be with; you sometimes never ever leave the city you start out in; when you're too old to turn a trick, it's already too late to get started in some other profession.

The way to succeed in hustling is really no big secret. It's the same as in every other business. You have to plan, work hard, and be lucky. The whole problem is that the majority of the people in the trade aren't there as businessmen. To be quite frank, they're there because of some emotional problem or problems. They probably shouldn't be into hustling at all. For the emotionally disturbed person, hustling usually offers no way to go but down.

According to Dr. George Henry, a psychiatrist whose work on the subject includes a discussion on homosexual prostitution in his *All the Sexes*, it appears that the majority of us hustlers are not homosexual by preference. We merely yield to homosexuality because hustling initially appears to be an easy and exciting way of maintaining ourselves. Like most delinquents, or offenders, we are rebellious against the law, authority, and the society in general. Half of male prostitutes, at least in Dr. Henry's study, had parents who were heavy drinkers. Several had been orphans before the age of ten. Many were from poverty-stricken homes.

Dr. Irving Bieber, in *Homosexuality: A Psychoanalytic Study*, is of the opinion that we homosexuals, in general, and we homosexual hustlers, in specific, are basically psychic masochists. Bieber feels that our homosexual adaptation is primarily the result of our hidden but incapacitating fears of the opposite sex.

When reading all such books, written by all such researchers, I, as a hustler, tend to take much of them with a grain of salt. Most of these good doctors have used a sampling of the hustling population which has come directly from the streets—an area which is at the bottom of the hustling barrel. Too many generalizations are often inferred from this minimum of information. This is not usually the doctors' fault, since most of them are actually trying to get valid information about a specific segment of society that isn't easily available to them. As a matter of fact, as inadequate as some of their deductions might be, I still commend the researchers, on the most part, for trying to examine an area that is hardly touched upon by scientific study even to this day. While female prostitution is much researched, male prostitution still exists beneath its veil of mystery and ignorance.

Male prostitution has increased substantially in the United States since World War I. Dr. Henry states that every major city has areas and places where men congregate for the purpose of selling favors. He estimates there must be a hundred thousand hustlers in greater New York City, alone; found in Times Square, Harlem, on Fifth Avenue, on Riverside Drive, in parks, in public toilets, on the waterfront, in baths, in restaurants, bars, nightclubs, and hotels; pretty much everywhere.

With that number of hustlers in that one area alone, it would seem inconceivable for definite statements to be made about male prostitution without first obtaining a far greater sampling of the hustling population than any doctor has so far been able to do. This inadequate sampling hasn't, of course, been the researchers' fault. As prostitution is against the law, and male prostitution is looked upon with even greater abhorrence than its female counterpart, adequate in-depth interviews with people in the trade are hard to come by.

Having been in the business a good many years, I, perhaps, have an insight none of the good researchers have had. I've met my fellow hustlers, talked with them, laughed with them, had gab sessions with them, fucked and sucked with them. To revamp a statement originally made about female prostitution in Bernard J. Oliver, Jr.'s *Sexual Deviation in American Society*: After a boy has gone into prostitution, he assumes the prostitute's special language and social role, fraternizing only with his peers. This cuts him off from the wider community and socially reinforces his resolve to remain in prostitution.

It is the general consensus of those researchers who have looked into the field that the majority of us male hustlers have inherent feelings of worthlessness, feel unwanted, unloved, and, therefore, seek affection and love through sex. To be succinct, the person into prostitution, like me, shows all indications of being more apt to be emotionally unbalanced than people in other professions.

Admitting that my own available sample group of the hustling population has given me access, perhaps, to more detailed information, it certainly couldn't be called any more representative of hustling, as a whole, than those samples taken by the good doctors. However, for what it's worth, it has led me to agree that hustling, by its very nature, attracts more than its share of mentally unstable people.

Most of my peers, familiar to me, within the business, come from broken homes, or from homes that had little warmth between parents. In their early lives, most hustlers I know were unable to achieve a basic attachment within the family unit.

Dr. Edward Glover suggests that prostitution is connected with the lack and/or deficiency of a love object.

Many hustlers, though, have problems often unrelated to prostitution, such as drug addition, and/or alcoholism. The majority isn't happy and feels degraded at having to submit to all forms of perversion for cash. Many of us feel resentful that our feelings are so seldom even considered by our clients, and feel that we are, as a result, used as inanimate sex objects, instead of as feeling human beings. Ten out of every fifteen hustlers I have known have tried to commit suicide at least once; three have succeeded.

Hustling has its mental pitfalls even for those of us who enter the profession with our eyes wide open and who aren't driven into the trade because of emotional hang-ups. Even some of us from normal homes, who lived comparatively normal lives, have found we've bitten off more than we can chew upon entering the body-selling business.

When I was living in a large apartment house on the East Coast, one of my clients asked me if knew my competition on the twenty-fifth floor. While I didn't even know the people who lived directly next door to me, at the time, Sam, the hustler upstairs, and I had actually met at a party on other side of town.

Sam was from a typically middle-class family. He had a brother who was a doctor, and a sister who was a housewife in suburbia. He had been to college, and he had majored in English. He had an apparently good relationship with his parents who thought he worked for a publishing company. I met Sam's mother and father, on more than one occasion, and they seemed to have a genuine affection for him, both as their son and as a person. Sam had his fits of depression, but seemingly no more than any of us did. He was good-looking, nicely put together, and had an adequate, if not enormous, cock. He had a steady clientele that stayed consistently at about five.

What impressed me most about him, however, was that he had researched hustling's potential for money-making before he had ever begun in the business. I looked upon him as a kindred spirit. He said he considered sex his livelihood and wasn't going to waste it on any non-productive relationships. Of all the people I've known in hustling, myself included, he seemed the most well-balanced. The chances are very good that I just imagined him that way, because it was important to me that I had seemingly found living verification that you can survive in our business without going off the deep end. I saw him basically as how I saw me, and still see me: someone who entered into the sex trade because it offers excellent potential, and not because we were neglected in childhood, were hated, or ignored, by unfeeling parents, were beaten and deprived of a necessary love object in adolescence, or were molested. Knowing why I entered hustling, but, also, aware that, by most anyone's standards, a hustler's life can hardly be considered normal, I wanted Sam as the reassurance he provided as a fellow survivor.

Thinking back, I can only remember one time when I must have seen him with his façade lowered, and that was only for a brief moment. He opened the door one evening and spent ten seconds just looking through me, rather than at me. It was a Tuesday night, and we usually took turns dropping by each other's apartment on those evenings to share a couple shots from a bottle of very-good Draqual Scotch. When he did recognize me, standing there, he gave the kind of smile that conveys anything but true amusement.

"Have you ever gotten tired, Malcomb?" he asked me. "I mean so fucking tired that you could give a goddamn whether the Earth stopped on its axis?"

I must have looked as surprised as I felt, because he laughed, this time with seemingly genuine amusement. The few seconds I'd seen him with his guard down had passed; I let them pass. I could have probably tried to get to the bottom of them, but I didn't. I'm convinced I really didn't want to know what was behind them. I wanted him just as I imagined him—competent, happy, and in complete control of his life and circumstances.

"I'm exhausted," he said, sitting down on the couch, facing me, his feet on the coffee table, and a glass of Scotch in his hand. I should have recognized that the exhaustion to which he referred, then, and the tiredness he had referred to at the door, were not one and the same thing. "I thought I was going to have my day completely free, to rest up, but Claymore called, this morning, to see if he could come over, and I told him to come ahead. His wife is pregnant, again, and he has an excuse to keep away from her. I think he only fucks her to get her pregnant so he can get away and get fucked by me."

He was, again, the Sam I knew; his "tiredness" and exhaustion acceptably explained away. His smile was back, and even the just-previous dark circles under his blue-gray eyes had somehow miraculously disappeared.

His shirt was open, revealing a vee of his hairless chest. His pants were tight and outlined his muscular legs and the length of his cock.

"I don't know where Claymore gets all of his energy," Sam continued. "He's a regular suck-and-fuck machine. This time, he brought around one of those books with illustrations of a couple corkscrewed into about six-hundred individual sexual positions. I thought he was going to have us duplicate every last one of them before he left. I feel like I've literally been tied into knots and put through the ringer.

"I had to get in full-lotus position. I didn't even know that I could manage it. Have you ever? Then, he sat down over my hard cock. The book said we should see how long we could stay that way without moving and/or ejaculating. He must have managed both for a whole two seconds." Sam laughed, again, and got up for a refill of Scotch. "I could hardly get my legs untangled afterwards.

"Another one of those positions instructed that I should throw my legs over my head and suck on my cock while I was humped by him from on top. My cock isn't nearly long big enough to let me eat it. Claymore didn't seem to give a damn.

"After that, we fucked in the shower. Then, I gave him an enema. He kept the tube shoved up his ass while I sat on his cock. Christ that was a riot!

"What he's always out to do, of course, is get me so fagged out that I'm starting to doubt I'll ever again manage another hard-on. Then, he makes me lie on the bed, and he starts licking. Thank God, he doesn't want me to try and get him hard, by that stage of any session; I'm so tired I couldn't even put up a show of even feigned interest in his prick.

"That's how it ends up just about every time he's with me. He did it even the first time we made it. In grand finale, he always just has me lie there, and do nothing, while he starts licking the soles of my feet, and then my toes. After those, he starts up my thigh to my cock. He doesn't touch my cock, then, though. He passes it on by, until he's licked to my chest where he starts biting on my nipples.

"He knows what he's doing. As tired as I always start out, my prick always starts getting hard, again, sooner or later, before he's through. Sometimes, I wish it wouldn't get hard, just so I could see Claymore's reaction, but it always does.

"After he does half the front of me, he starts at my face and does the other half. Then, he turns me over, does even more licking, and ends up eating out my ass. My God, that guy has the longest tongue of anyone I know. He sticks it so far up my butt; I sometimes think he's let a snake loose in my asshole. Actually, I think he gets that baby poked in all of the way to my prostate. By, then, of course, my cock is usually genuinely rock-hard.

"When he's through sucking my ass clean, he rolls me to my back, and climbs up and over me into a dominant sixty-nine position. You know what I have to do, then, while he grazes on my cock that one final time? I have to bite his nuts. The way he's kneeling over me, all I have to do is open my mouth, and his nuts are right there. He sucks my dick, and I bite his balls. And, I mean, he really wants me to bite those babies—hard. Big mothers they are, too.

"Sometimes, he goes all the way down on my dick, and he even sucks my balls into his hungry face. Then, he sticks out that long snaky tongue of his and sends it far enough, down beneath my dick, actually to reach my asshole. I swear to God, I haven't a clue how he does it.

"Nor do I ever have a clue as to from where I always, somehow, manage to come up with those last gut-jarring shots of cum I always feed him. He always brags that he gets more out of my nuts that last time than he ever does during the first part of our sessions. I think he's full of shit.

"It's always a wild cum for me, though: that last one. I'm always surprised when I feel it on its way. And it's never like the others. It has a certain painful quality to it— more pleasure, though, than pain, if you know what I mean. My balls are usually sore (although not as sore, I would assume, as Claymore's balls from my gnawing at them).

"'Bite me!' it always sounds as if he squeals. Of course, I can't tell what the hell he's really saying, because his mouth is always so full of my cock shooting my exploding cum.

"Anyway, whatever he's asking for, if anything, I bite his balls—both of them—the hardest yet. Every damned time, right on cue, his nuts bust. His cum isn't thick or runny. It's a hot splattering of gelatinous dollops that end up stuck to my chest and belly.

"I wonder what makes Claymore tick. You ever wonder about your johns, Malcomb? What in God's name makes any of them tick? What makes us tick for that matter?"

In June of last year, I got back from a two-week stay, with a client, on St. Thomas in the Caribbean. Sam had committed suicide while I was gone; hanged himself by a robe cord from a towel rack in his bathroom. No evidence of a struggle; his valuables and money were all around, a lot of them in full view.

He left a suicide note, of sorts; just two words written with black-felt pen on a piece of very expensive cream-colored stationery:

I'm tired!

ALEX

Anyone of us into hustling, with even the basic psychology and/or sociology school courses under his belt, can recognize the many similarities to be drawn between male and female prostitution. Many female whores come from broken homes, were unwanted in adolescence, had one or more drunken parent, have inherent feelings of unworthiness, have drug or alcohol problems, were abused and even molested. I know many of my fellow male hustlers who can easily fit into one or more of those same categories.

There is one specific area, however, where the two, male and female, seem, pretty much always, drastically to differ.

Half of the women in a sample of twenty, mentioned by Bernard J. Oliver, Jr., in his *Sexual Deviation in American Society*, were reported to be totally frigid in their customer relationships; eighteen with almost no sexual feelings at all. "They deny their frigidity by faking all the uninhibited aspects of having an orgasm."

We men, however, cannot make it in the trade if we're unable to get a hard-on, maintain that erection, and eventually ejaculate. Our customers cannot be fooled by any amount of acted enthusiasm and desire when our limp penes tell them otherwise. And while male orgasm can sometimes be faked, usually during anal intercourse by the hustler in the dominant position, I doubt anyone ever got to the top of the hustling ladder with non-cum-producing cock and balls.

Unlike a woman, whose sexual spasms are not accompanied by the ejaculation of sperm (despite what is often read in heterosexual and/or lesbian fuck books), our climaxes are out there for one and all to see. Women take cocks up her cunts, moan, groan, scream, "I cum!" and who's to prove otherwise? Are we going to get away with such a charade, though? It's not likely, because there are just too many visible indications of our degrees of sexual excitement for us to do so.

So, while our female counterparts apparently make the grade with a lifetime of simulated passion and orgasm, we seem doomed if we attempts to follow in their footsteps.

The mistake of many laymen is to assume that since all this appears quite reasonable, it must, then, follow that we're apparently afflicted by satyriasis. Such an assumption is absurd! A hustler who has an uncontrollable or excessive desire for intercourse, which is the definition for satyriasis, isn't a serious hustler, at all, in that his main concern is his sexual satisfaction and not the financial rewards to be gained from it.

Another hasty laic assumption is that we are, by necessity, promiscuous. Again wrong! A promiscuous person, by definition, advocates a confused and/or indiscriminate mingling. Most of us never go to bed with just anybody if we can help it.

Such misinterpretations invariably occur because of the very nature of the business. Sex is bought and sold; therefore, it is easily assumed that sex must be the predominant concern of all of us involved. I have known cases where this was true; there are, indeed, half-assed hustlers who are apt to go for free sex if they can't find anyone willing to pay for it.

None of us, though, make it to the pinnacle of the hustling hierarchy by giving our services away. Nor do we make it to the top with sex as our primary goal. Sex to us is a means of attaining some other end: money, gifts, travel, and etcetera.

Many of us big-time hustlers are neither satyrs, nor are we promiscuous. We're not even oversexed. Rather, we're a special hybrid whose frigidity differs only from our prostitute sisters in that it is accompanied with an erection, with ejaculate, and even with a certain degree of excitation achieved during orgasm.

We successful male prostitutes are closer to Bernard Oliver's observations of our female equivalents than might have seemed possible at first glance. While we're not totally frigid—if one is to assume male frigidity denotes complete impotency—we aren't the norm, either, even by homosexual standards. Most of us who make it really big are, from birth or though training, able to somehow dissociate ourselves from certain basic emotional drives natural in most other men.

I was never plagued by my sexual drive as much as everyone else seemed to be. Even at puberty, I didn't feel a desire to get into some girl's or boy's pants. I was content to jack off. I talked about laying girls, but I didn't have sexual intercourse with one until I was in the military. Even that wasn't spontaneous.

Where I was stationed in the service, there was quite a large homosexual community. All the latest information about which queer private was doing what, with which corporal, or which colonel was screwing which lieutenant, was somehow eventually always filtered down to me.

"You know, Alex," this one gay sergeant said to me, "even if you aren't queer, and even I don't know that for sure...." Meaning, if he didn't know, then, no one did. "...you'd still be one of the first to get a 209 dishonorable discharge in case of a purge. You know too damned much about what does go on, here, gay-wise, ever to be seen as just an innocent bystander."

About that time, I realized one of the American civilians attached to the military was sexually interested in me. I figured, since I was going to be suspected of being a queer anyway, I might as well reap some of the benefits.

Do you know what I did to prepare myself for my proposed liaison with this guy? I arranged, through a friend and fellow solider of mine, to fuck a female whore. I had no desire to fuck one, but I thought it would be something to fall back on if I were later accused of being queer. Funny thing is, I ended up fucking the whore and never got around to doing anything with the civilian. Not that I found cunt so great that it turned me exclusively straight, because it didn't; in fact, far from it.

I doubt I've ever had a genuinely satisfactory sexual relationship, period—with any man or with any woman. Oh, I've never had any problems getting an erection or ejaculating. However, I seem continually to be playing the scientist, looking objectively upon all of my sexual experiences, and analyzing them, even while they're in progress.

I think I could get an erection and have sex with anything, or anybody, if the price was right. I don't even have to like the person or the thing. I merely tell myself that I'm going to need an erection, to do what I have to do, and one pops up automatically between my legs. It was there for the prostitute, and it was there for Mallory. With neither did I feel any great gut-burning desire. Nor have I ever.

Mallory was my first trick as a hustler, even though I had no inclinations, at the time, that I would soon be the professional I am today. He was young, attractive, and, as it turned out, definitely interested. We were at one of those parties where most everyone is either homosexual or bisexual, and in the theater. I got into that scene like I seem to get into everything else gay: by accident. I had just been discharged (honorably, by the way) from the Army and moved into an apartment. Immediately, I was discovered by a gay neighbor who thought I knew "the score." The neighbor's name was Sven. Sven got me invited to the party where I met Mallory.

Mallory asked me if I wanted to go home with him and have sex. I said no. After which, he sent Sven over for a chat.

"Mallory has been asking about you, Alex," Sven said. "He knows a lot of people. His father has been an angel for a lot of major plays." I was so new to it all, at the time, that I thought Mallory's old man used to fly across the stage wearing tinsel wings (à la Peter Pan) whenever there was a part that called for it. When I found out how many Broadway shows have been launched with that guy's money, I still feel a little ridiculous. "I told Mallory," Sven continued, "that he shouldn't take your rejection personally, because you're a hustler." Then, he looked at me really queer-like and said, "You are a hustler, Alex." It wasn't a question. I told him, yes, because I thought it would get him and Mallory off my case.

That wasn't the case, though. Mallory came over, again, and, this time, asked how much I charged for an evening. I thought he was joking and came up with what I thought was a pretty fantastic price. Imagine my surprise when, without blinking an eye, he opened his wallet and counted out the cash, then and there. I found out later, he'd inherited a pile of money from his grandmother, plus the substantial monthly allowance he got from his parents at the time.

We went to his place.

I played the hustler role we'd assigned me, getting undressed while he made us drinks. I had a hard-on; as if Mallory was the Army officer who had requisitioned it, and I was the supply sergeant who, as ordered, had brought it on: nothing more, nothing less.

I asked him if he wanted to fuck me in the ass in the bedroom, or right there on the floor. He asked me what made me think he wanted to fuck me at all. I shrugged and told him for the price he was paying I was sure he didn't have me there for small talk. My real indifference must have come through, because he didn't even smile. He did strip, though, and probably expected me to go ape-shit over his exceptional body. It was, indeed, nicely muscled and probably had a lot of normal queers going all gaga over it. I wasn't a normal queer, however; I found it, and him, more interesting than exciting.

"I do want to fuck you," he said.

No shit, Sherlock! Then, I wondered aloud, "What if I want to fuck you?"

"It's my money paying for this party," he reminded. "So, how about you just push your naked belly into that couch over there?"

I told him he could have his money back. That threw him for a loop. Then, I said, "Or, maybe, when I'm done fucking your ass, you won't want me to give you your money back." I went over and kissed him. It was the first time I'd ever kissed a man. It didn't really do much for me; I would have thought he could tell my lack of experience, enjoyment, and sincerity, but it didn't seem to happen.

We ended up wrestling our way to the couch, he down on it belly-first, only putting up token protest to me trying to get my cock lined up for a successful push up his asshole.

"God, yes, oh, God, yes!" was what he mumbled when I finally did stick his ass with all nine thick inches of my hard cock; his sphincter was suddenly gummed tightly around the circumference of my prick base.

I pulled eight of my nine inches free and, then, rammed them all home, once again. Simultaneously, I worked my hands beneath his chest. His nipples were like tacks against my palms.

I pumped him for a good twenty minutes. I began to feel an impending climax, but it wasn't anything pressing.

I could tell the second he popped his rocks, because his asshole started to spasm about my prick, like crazy; he started squealing accompaniment. Frankly, my not having provided him with any play-time for his cock, and him never having physically taken hold of it, I was surprised he got off with only my fucking his butt.

When he was finished letting loose onto the couch cushions beneath him, he seemed surprised to find me still hard inside him. It seemed to worry him, but I told him I usually held off ejaculation for as long as it took for a customer to get off.

"Could you cum, though, if I blew you?"

I couldn't imagine anyone wanting to eat a cock that had been just been plugged up his butt, but it was his suggestion, not mine.

"Hey, I'm a hustler, right? It's what the customer wants; even if he may mistakenly, initially, think he wants his dick inside me, instead of vice versa."

"Let's do it, then," he said.

I could have ejaculated up his butt in just a couple more seconds, with just a couple more pumps, and a bit more concentration, if I'd really set my mind to it, but he seemed anxious to suck me, so….

I pulled out my dick and stood by the side of the couch. He came to a sitting position on one cum-dampened cushion.

He started off by licking my balls and continued on up my cock belly, all of the way to my cock head. Then, he swallowed a good six inches of my prick with a resounding gulp. Quickly, thereafter, he siphoned up all my remaining cock inches as completely as his asshole had managed the very same thing.

His lips moved slowly up and down my boner, traveling from the thick, vein-bulged base to the fist-sized corona. Suddenly, his mouth held only the crown of my cock, and his tongue probed my dick meatus for some of its salty pre-cum discharge. For me, the experience wasn't completely devoid of pleasure; I could likely cum in his mouth if that was what he wanted.

I grabbed his head, letting my hands ride with it over my dick, rather than actually direct its movements. I tightened my ass and leg muscles which usually hastens climax for me. Mallory grabbed my balls and squeezed. I obliged him with a mouthful of sperm. I groaned, not because I had any great need to do so, but because I assumed he would expect some such verbal response.

Then, I let him fuck me, figuring turnabout was fair play. Besides, I think that he so pressed for it to happen in order to prove some vague point about his manhood.

Later that evening, he told me he could see why I asked the price I did, in that I was "so damned hot and so fucking good."

We saw each other over the next three years. He introduced me to a lot of people and taught me a lot, in and out of bed, without even knowing it. He never really understood me, though, and never even knew he was the first guy with whom I'd ever had paid sex; to this day, I don't know if that makes me happy or sad.

Mallory considered me an experienced hustler up until the very end of our relationship. It was from him that I first heard that ridiculous question about whether or not I thought all of my years of sucking and fucking affected my normal sex life and drives.

You know how I answered him? I said the same thing I answered the asshole who asked me that very same question, later, when I did have years of paid sucking and fucking to my credit. I said, "What in the hell makes you think a hustler, any hustler, ever had a normal sex life, or drives, to begin with?"

Most of my fellow successful hustlers aren't controlled by their sex drives. How in the hell could any of us ever get anywhere in this fucking business if we were controlled by our goddamned cocks and balls like normal people? Right?

CAL (AND PETER)

I had my first homosexual experience at eighteen. I let a tennis pro at the country club suck my cock for $50. Of course, I knew I was gay way before then. I just didn't know, until the tennis pro, that selling my cock and ass had such potential as money-earners.

I'm now twenty-six. Not all of my money, these days, comes from just selling my body. I've made several good investments over the years. I have a degree in business administration. I speak five languages, fluently, and can read two more. For the past few years, I've been living in Japan.

If you want to hustle for money (or, more appropriately "for yen"), some Japanese men still have plenty of it, and they can be very generous with it, not to mention be dedicated and loyal lovers. Unfortunately, or fortunately, they, also, have a tendency to get emotionally involved. A hustler everywhere, especially here, must avoid emotional involvement unless he's capable of handling it intelligently as part of his overall long-range game-plan.

Those of us into hustling haven't got forever to make our marks. Our working years are damned few. Maybe, we have only until we're thirty to make the grade. If we have made it by then, there's the possibility (if we've been smart, have a devoted clientele, and have been taking good care of ourselves, physically and mentally), we might even extend our work-time for another five years. However, even with that possibly too generously an assumed terminus of any hustler's actual viability on the market place, it still leaves us damned little time to get set up for retirement. Any years of non-monetary emotional involvement taken out of our limited productive period can mean less chance for our ever achieving old-age security.

One person I know, who had all the right chances for success in this business, fell in love with a top bank executive. They lived together for three years before the inevitable break-up. This hustler ended up with nothing for his time and effort but a broken heart, an overworked mouth and asshole, and three years taken out of his prime.

I'm not suggesting we should shove all of our emotions into a drawer for fifteen or so years and, then, conveniently, pull them out, again, when our money-making years as male prostitutes have—so to speak—all petered out; although, that's not a bad suggestion for me to make. If we fall in love, we had better temper that love with some practicality and common sense. We must make sure we take out some insurance against that love going sour. We can't afford to let love affairs interfere with our projected goals.

Every successful hustler I know has a time-table. He knows his final goal and how far he has progressed towards it. If he "gets married", or "involved", then he still sticks to his original plan. He makes sure his husband/wife/lover gives him cash, stocks, bonds, or some other form of tangible compensation for the income he would be making elsewhere.

Sound unromantic? It probably does, and it probably is, but at least it gives us something to fall back on if, or when, we're suddenly left high and dry. If a relationship is going to last forever, there's no harm in ferreting away a little nest egg, just in case. If it doesn't last forever, or even for a year or two, that little nest egg will, at least, hopefully, eventually, make it all seem worthwhile. Divorce between men, after all, doesn't require any division of existing property, unless it's done in one of the few places where same-sex marriages are legal and binding.

Peter is another very successful hustler, besides me, here, in Japan. He and I last met during business negotiations conducted, earlier this year, between my john, Paul, and Peter's john, Yukio, as regarded the possibilities of Paul's American headquarters obtaining exclusive U.S. distribution rights for a line of innovative electronic products developed by the Japanese company in which Yukio is employed. Paul, also, previously knew Yukio from their Harvard days when they'd tricked together.

Having begun hustling at eighteen, Peter says he'll retire at thirty. I believe him. Like I did, he attained all of his considerable capital without the help of a syndicate or underworld influences. He did it by formulating his own business plan and following through on it.

If even a small percentage of us who enter the profession could have any real chance of reaching the goals Peter and I have, I suspect there would be a vast influx of bodies-for-sale introduced onto the playing field.

I have some ideas why Peter and I have reached the big time in our profession, while not everyone else, who has joined us in pulling down his pants, has done as well.

Certainly, there are plenty of people with bigger cocks than ours, better looks than ours, better and tighter assholes than ours. I think success in this business, though, goes deeper than anything physical. A john with money, established in his career and social strata, isn't necessarily looking just for sex. Sex is an important part, of course, but there's also a need for companionship, and a need for someone to talk to who can utter more than mundane one- or two-syllable words. The term, since I'm in Japan, which comes most immediately to mind, is "male-geisha."

Let's face it; two-thirds of us in hustling, no matter where we are in the world, don't have the opportunity to meet the gay men who have lots of money. Not many *uber*-rich clients cruise the street corners, or the local K-Marts, or the baths, or gay bars. Rather, they're found in certain posh neighborhoods, at certain private clubs, laughing and talking with their equally wealthy peers. Most of us who have access to the moneyed people of this world, as a chance of making a great success of male prostitution, already have money and don't need to bother, or we have the smarts and connections to succeed in some other line of business, which is usually what the majority of us do.

One big mistakes made by us, I think, is that we become too enmeshed in the homosexual world, other than just in its necessary sexual aspects. It's surprising how few straight friends the lower- and middle-grade hustlers seem to have. However, most of the people with money have made it in the straight world. Whether or not these wealthy men have homosexual tendencies, they exist primarily within a heterosexual environment. Homosexual men with money work in heterosexual offices, go to heterosexual clubs, associate with heterosexual people who belong to the heterosexual majority. Often, gay men with money hide their homosexuality beneath the guise of a heterosexual wife and family. If these men are going to make it with us, it's important we—as much as possible—be able to alleviate whatever fears these major closet cases have regarding the continued survival of their carefully constructed façades. It takes only one indiscretion, or one indiscreet person, to throw a monkey-wrench into the whole works.

Therefore, it's my firm belief that it is of great importance that we be able, freely and comfortably, to exist within the heterosexual stratum. The best way for us to get to a gay man with money is to know his friends with money and go to the places where he and his money go.

I met Paul, an American, through Mildred. Mildred is a widow who is one of the leading figures in what's left of Japan's American colony. Paul has a wife and three kids. I've met his wife, and she's really quite charming.

We have to be able to handle ourselves with women, even flirt with them so that they don't suspect we're possible competition. We have to be good actors. We have to be able to pretend we're having a good time even if we aren't. We have to be able to pretend the two-inch cocks up our butts are the biggest and best we've ever taken. We have to be able to pretend assholes, even if more spacious than any barns, are the tightest things our dicks ever fucked. We have to pretend we find people attractive when we really find them junk-yard-dog ugly.

Paul didn't immediately become a regular client of mine, nor did we hop right into bed, that day I was first introduced to him. At the time, I wasn't really even sure he was gay. I merely had a suspicion. We acquire an intuition for identifying potential customers (gaydar?), or for leads to potential customers.

I arranged to go to the same spa to which Paul belonged. I made it a point to work out with him. Eventually, he started taking me around to his club. He introduced me to even more people: American, European, and Oriental. The more people we know—gay and straight—the better. If we know people who know people who are good friends of the Bradleys, then we have an edge, right there, for starting up a conversation with Mr. Bradley whose partner is a possible client.

Only after we grew completely comfortable with each other, did Paul and I enter into our present ongoing pay-for-sex business relationship that had me along when he and his old friend, Yukio, talked business punctuated by a bit of hustlers-bought-and-paid-for (Peter and I) entertainment.

During one of Paul and Yukio's longer negotiation sessions, Peter and I gravitated to one of the bedrooms of the hotel suite that had been booked for the meeting. Paul and Yukio were confident enough of their Alpha positions not to pay us much mind. It was highly unlikely that we, their two purchased hustlers, would prove unprofessional enough to jilt the men who'd hired us, even if we did play around with each other when neither Paul nor Yukio needed our immediate services. Certainly, neither Peter nor I, for a moment, thought we would, either. It isn't that we aren't physically attracted to each other, but, rather, that we both have projected time-tables into which neither of us fits the other, over the long run; only for the short run of some peripheral, then and there, fun and games before taking up, again, with our presently occupied-elsewhere-for-the-moment paying clients.

Finished with very enjoyable dual orgasms that weren't likely to keep our cocks down and out for very long, accomplished while leisurely sixty-nining on one of the bedroom's two king-size beds, Peter and I were naked and still breathing hard when Paul and Yukio came in, pretty much ignored us, except for passing nods, stripped down (don't ever let anyone convince you that all Oriental cock is small cock), and laid out, side-by-side, on the bed opposite.

Quickly, though, Yukio moved to kneel between Paul's splayed legs. Yukio's head bowed, and his tongue flicked outward and washed first one of Paul's nipples and, then, the other.

The dimness of the lighting in the room made their bodies, one white, one golden, seem sensuously blurred. Their swollen cocks, one white, one golden, seemed large and bulky. I could feel Peter's body against mine; our breathing, never completely calmed after our orgasms, got more and more rapid as we played voyeurs.

Paul and Yukio kissed: mouth-on-mouth, cock-on-cock. Their cheeks ballooned and, then, concaved as their tongues probed and shared spit.

Yukio worked his knees under Paul's upper legs. He pulled Paul's lower body closer until Paul's butt was mashed against Yukio's healthy nuts. Yukio's hard-on jutted from his lower belly, looming so far upward past Paul's balls that its head almost touched the apex of Paul's prick when Yukio pried the latter upward from his companion's hard belly. Yukio's hands wrapped the suddenly joined, belly-to-belly, phallic poles and commenced a hearty masturbation of the two.

Yukio bent from his waist until his face hovered over the pre-cum drooling double-domes of beat meat. His tongue lapped the top of Paul's erection. His mouth fell and then swallowed first the top of Paul's dick and, then, the tip of Yukio's dick.

Eventually, Yukio's face pulled away, and he placed his arms under Paul's thighs to lift Paul's legs around Yukio's neck. Paul's large pecker jabbed the folds of his pale American businessman's belly.

Yukio's prick, its tip still wet from his sucking of it, and from additional oozing of pre-seminal juice, was shiny from its thick corona to halfway down its neck.

Paul's legs secured, Yukio's hands pressed open the crack of Paul's creamy ass, revealing the sweat-moistened valley that was punctuated by its darkly winked anal pucker.

Yukio's right hand positioned his dick on the target; his left hand kept Paul's ass cheeks separated. Once his swollen phallus was in place, he pressed his pelvis forward and buried his cock's thick head within the enfolding sphincter. The walls of the buttocks closed in on the prick's jabbing. Yukio's fingers grabbed handfuls of hard

American businessman's ass as Paul's asshole slipped farther and farther over the penetrating Japanese penis that Yukio continued to feed it.

Paul grabbed his cock and groaned loudly in announcement of Oriental erection colliding with Occidental prostate within the depths of his asshole. His hand-held meat drooled pre-cum that he smeared along its vein-latticed length with a pumping motion that quickly achieved the same easy rhythm that Yukio assumed in fucking Paul's willing asshole.

They didn't climax in that position. Before they let their orgasms shudder through them, they moved and shifted several times: Yukio drew his cock free only to assume doggie position and take on Paul's hard cock; Yukio rolled to his back, Paul sunk his ass over Yukio's uplifted prick and pumped his own fisted boner.

When they finally did climax, they did so, simultaneously, in a sixty-nine position on the bed, just as Peter and I had done on our bed before them: their hungry mouths sank completely over their throbbing sex-meats, their hungry throats contracted spasmodically about their emptying male dicks, and their sweat-shined bodies seemed equally set aglow.

Peter and I, definitely aroused by what we'd seen and saw, rolled into a face-to-face, belly-to-belly, cock-to-cock embrace. Shortly, Yukio and Paul, no more satiated by their comes than Peter and I been made by ours, joined us on our bed.

People have asked me if hustlers like Peter and I are really happy. What do I answer? Only that: we each have a yearly income in the six figures. We have fat portfolios of long-term stocks and bonds, small fortunes in contemporary art. Between us, we own a town house in London, a flat in Paris, two condos in San Francisco and one in Acapulco. We've reached the pinnacle of our profession, where many aspire to be but where few end up being.

ABOUT THE AUTHOR

WILLIAM MALTESE, the internationally bestselling author of novels, short story collections, and his popular Stud Draqual Mystery Series, has published (under various pseudonyms) close to two hundred books in genres including gay and straight erotica, sci-fi, science-fantasy, mystery, romance, western, adventure, espionage, cooking, wine, and children. With a Business/Advertising degree, Maltese enlisted in the U.S. Army, where he achieved and was honorably discharged at a Sergeant (E-5) rank. Presently, he divides his time between the Pacific Northwest and New York City. You can visit his websites at:

www.williammaltese.com
www.myspace.com/williammaltese
www.facebook.com/williammaltese

www.ingramcontent.com/pod-product-compliance
Lightning Source LLC
Chambersburg PA
CBHW050750250626
47155CB00005B/2003